SECRETS OF A
HAUNTED
WINTER

SECRETS OF A
HAUNTED
WINTER

BRENDAN GRIFFIN

www.brendangriffinbooks.com

First published in 2014 by
Brendan Griffin
www.brendangriffinbooks.com
Keel, Castlemaine, Co. Kerry, Ireland.
Tel: 00353 85 889 2939
info@brendangriffinbooks.com

ISBN: 978-0-9931437-0-0

Typesetting and design by Fairways Design
www.fairwaysdesign.com

Printed and bound by Walsh Colour Print, Tralee Road, Castleisland,
Co. Kerry, Ireland.

Front and back cover image by Cathy Giles, Ardcanaught,
Castlemaine, Co. Kerry, Ireland.

Internal illustrations by Brendan Griffin.

This book may be purchased online at
www.brendangriffinbooks.com

A CIP catalogue record for this book is available from
the British Library.

For my father and mother, Michael and Betty, for all the good
things you have done…

CONTENTS

Acknowledgements   ix

Foreword   xii

Prologue – Bad News   1

Chapter 1 – Making Amends   3

Chapter 2 – Discovery   9

Chapter 3 – A Story for the Road   20

Chapter 4 – A Big Day Out   29

Chapter 5 – Mass   31

Chapter 6 – Back on the Water   38

Chapter 7 – Prime Suspects   42

Chapter 8 – The Plan   51

Chapter 9 – Placing the Order   58

Chapter 10 – A Village Divided   61

Chapter 11 – A Lead   66

Chapter 12 – Action   76

Chapter 13 – More Bad News   80

Chapter 14 – The Great Escape   82

Chapter 15 – The Beautiful Light 92

Chapter 16 – The Woods at Night 94

Chapter 17 – The Ballycastle Derby 95

Chapter 18 – Alright on the Night 104

Chapter 19 – What Billy Did 111

Chapter 20 – What Barty Did 113

Chapter 21 – What Garda Jim Did 115

Chapter 22 – What Granda & Cathal Did 117

Chapter 23 – Donkey & Chicken 119

Chapter 24 – Piecing the Clues Together 123

Chapter 25 – Closure 128

Epilogue 130

St. Joseph's NS Christmas
Fundraising Concert Programme 131

ACKNOWLEDGEMENTS

There are so many of you that I am truly grateful to for your assistance with *Secrets of a Moonlit River* and *Secrets of a Haunted Winter*.

In no particular order, here goes:

To my family and friends, thank you for your encouragement, feedback on early drafts and, very importantly, your proofing assistance – Paddy Clifford, Eoghan Murphy, Kieran Houlihan, Mike Griffin, Kelly McMorrow, Judy McMorrow, Tommy Griffin, Sinéad Griffin, Dominick Clifford, Avril Cronin and Aimee Griffin – Thank you for <u>spotitng</u> all the errors!

To Cathy and Kevin Giles, thank you for giving me the kick that I needed to pursue matters and for helping to bring my work to a wider readership. Cathy, you are a wonderful artist, as the cover image of this book proves.

To Richard Moriarty, I admire your enthusiasm to place these local books on the global stage…no limits!!!

To Seán Kelly, MEP, thank you for performing the official launch of *Secrets of a Moonlit River* and for taking time out from your hectic schedule to say nice things about me and my writing!

To all of the organisers of the Keel Christmas Market, especially Ger O'Dowd - for your beautiful backdrop, thank you for facilitating my launches and for your Trojan community efforts – they'd be fierce lucky to have ye in Ballycastle!

To Ray Carpenter, thank you for photographing the launch of *Secrets of a Moonlit River*. Your photographs are always pleasant supplements to fond memories.

To all of my former teachers at Castledrum National School and the Intermediate School, Killorglin, thank you for your help and dedication over the years, especially my English teacher, Jim O'Malley, for planting the notion in a lazy teenager's mind that he might someday write for fun!

To the members of local and national media, thank you for reviewing and publicising my writing – and for being gentle with me!

To all of the retailers who agreed to stock my books, thank you for your kindness and your valuable shelf space!

To Tony Walsh and all of your dedicated team at Walsh Colour Print, thank you for your efficiency and professionalism at all times. I'm delighted to be printing in Kerry!

To Glen McArdle, Fairways Design, thank you for your exquisitely tasteful work on layout and covers and for your speed and flexibility.

To Bridget McAuliffe, Red Hen Publishing, thank you so much for getting me started with your invaluable assistance throughout *Secrets of a Moonlit River* and for showing me the process of producing a book.

To my son, Micheál, thank you for being such a good sleeper during our holidays, allowing Daddy some time to get his books edited. I really look forward to your feedback when you are old enough to read them.

To my wife, Róisín, thank you for your patience and understanding over the years, while your boyfriend/fiancé/husband spent time with manuscripts instead of with his girlfriend/fiancée/wife…I'm a very lucky man!

Finally but not least, to you the reader, thank you for supporting my work – every word that's written is done with your enjoyment in mind.

FOREWORD

There's something very special about meeting people who have read and enjoyed your novel. For me, the most rewarding experience with *Secrets of a Moonlit River* was visiting a particular school and seeing the enthusiasm on the faces of the children. This was the first group of children who had read my book as their class novel. To a debut novelist, it was highly encouraging to be on the receiving end of probing and thoughtful questions about plot, characters, themes and setting.

One of the main reasons it took so long for *Secrets of a Moonlit River* to see the light of day was my fear of rejection. Even up to the day of its launch, I still harboured fears and misgivings about "going public" with my writing! I just hoped that people would enjoy the story being told. When the first reviews started coming back, I breathed a heavy sigh of relief, but it was the children excitedly asking - "when is the next book coming out?" - that really meant the most to me.

So, here it is. I give you *Secrets of a Haunted Winter*. Like its predecessor, most of this story was written during 2007 and 2008, usually after finishing work in the early hours of the morning, on a bar counter in a deserted *Castle Inn*, Castlemaine. A few days of editing on my holidays during the glorious summer of 2014 was all it took to finish the job and I am delighted to finally have all of my *Ballycastle* adventures out in the open!

This is a story, nothing more or nothing less. Wherever and whenever you may be reading it, I hope it brings you enjoyment.

Warm regards,
Brendan Griffin
November 2014

BAD NEWS

Granda turned on the kitchen radio just in time for the morning news.

Good morning, you're listening to Kingdom FM, it's 8 o'clock on Monday, December 16th, 2013. Here is the news:

Gardaí in Killcrown are investigating a burglary at a residence in the locality, which took place sometime between 3pm yesterday and 11pm last night.

It is understood that many valuable items, including antiques and paintings, were taken from the house while the owner was not at home.

Gardaí are appealing to members of the public for any information that may assist their inquiries. In particular, they are looking for information on anyone that may have been seen acting suspiciously in the Murphy's Estate and Murphy's Woods area at any time yesterday. Witnesses are asked to contact Killcrown Garda Station.

∼

In community news, the Ballycastle Parish Christmas Fundraising Concert will take place on Saturday, December 21st at 8pm in Ballycastle Community Hall. All funds raised will go to repairing the church roof. People are asked to give generously, as there is a big hole in the roof just above the choir gallery.

~

Finally, in births, deaths and marriages, Michael McNamara of Ballycastle Road, Killcrown, has passed away in his 107th year. Rumours had circulated last week that Michael was dead but these were untrue. It has emerged that Michael suffered a heart attack after hearing the rumours and passed away last night. For funeral details and all the other news stories, tune in to the main morning news at 9 o'clock. It's just gone a minute past eight.

Granda promptly turned off the radio.

"There's never anything important on that 'aul wireless!" he thought.

CHAPTER 1
MAKING AMENDS

M orale was low in Murphy's Woods.

"How many more?" Cathal asked wearily, as he stuck his spade in the ground and rested his tired upper body on the handle.

"I reckon we've about sixty planted, just a few more to go," responded the industrious Billy from the far end of a zone of freshly planted sapling trees.

"How many are left in the trailer?" Cathal shouted to Barty, whose chief responsibility was to draw the saplings from a car trailer to where Billy and Cathal were working their spades. The trailer was parked on the roadside, not far from the planting place. However, Barty, not renowned for his love of hard labour, had by now abandoned his task and had taken respite in a quiet corner of the plantation. There he sat on a rock, drinking lukewarm tea from a plastic bottle whilst simultaneously rummaging in his back sack, searching for the bar of chocolate that he had packed that morning.

"Hi, Barty, get your rear in gear and help us get finished," shouted Billy to his younger brother with frustration.

"Alright, alright, calm down," Barty shouted back, as he hastily returned to work with the chocolate bar in his hand. "I only took a break for a minute."

"How many to go Barty?" asked Cathal again.

"About twenty."

"Oh man, we'll be another hour at least," Cathal observed despairingly, as he dug another hole in the coarse and boggy ground.

"Well, my mastermind brother should have thought of this long before now," remarked Barty, as he carried a new bundle of saplings towards Cathal, his remark being directed towards Billy.

"You were at it too fool," Billy sniped back from a distance.

"Yea, but it was your idea Billy."

"You went along with it Fatty."

"Don't call me Fatty Billy!"

"I didn't call you Fatty Billy, I just called you Fatty!"

"Billy, I swear to God I'll come over there to you!"

"And what?"

"Okay, lads okay," interjected Cathal. "Shut it for goodness sake. We'll never get finished at this rate. Can we just concentrate on getting this done and get out of here? It's past three o'clock at this stage."

His intervention had the desired effect and the boys got back to work.

Cathal was anxious to get the job finished and was fed up to be planting trees on a Saturday. The experience had left him absolutely determined not to have to spend Sunday doing it too. It was December 14th, and while most other people were in town, Christmas shopping or enjoying the Ballycastle Christmas Market in the nearby village, Cathal and the Shanahan brothers were busy planting. Earlier that morning, Cathal's grandfather, with whom he had been living for only a few weeks, since the death of his parents and brother, had driven the three boys to Murphy's Woods, pulling the car trailer full of young trees, which he had bought at a nearby nursery for the planting project.

Planting the final twenty trees proved to be hard work, with Cathal and Billy's hands beginning to blister from friction with the spade handle, and Barty's back aching from all the bending and lifting. At one stage, Cathal came across what appeared to be an old piece of cloth buried in the soil. He thought this to be quite unusual and instinctively put the piece of cloth in his pocket and continued working. By the time the last tree was put in the soil, evening was quickly closing in and soon the boys were working in twilight. Although they had been in Murphy's Woods in complete darkness before, they still felt a distinct unease about being there, regardless of whether it was day or night. There was just something strange about those woods that gave it a creepy and unwelcoming feeling.

"That's the last one," declared Barty, as Billy worked the spade for the final time. "I don't know about ye lads but I'm not hanging around here for a minute longer," he added, unashamedly admitting his dislike of the woods.

"Same as that," agreed Cathal. "And I certainly don't like the way that layer of fog has come down along by the river."

"That's so weird," remarked Billy. "I'd swear that it wasn't there a minute ago."

"And it's coming our way now," exclaimed Barty, pointing to the thick wave of fog that was now rapidly moving inland from the banks of the nearby River Clane, sweeping over Murphy's Woods, and plunging the area where the boys were working into near-darkness in a matter of moments.

"Oh my God, that's so creepy," said Cathal, with fear in his voice. "It's like something from a horror movie. I've never seen anything like that before."

"Oh me and Barty have," replied Billy. "Sometimes it just comes in there quicker than you could ever imagine. It happened to us one night while we were crossing the river in the boat, before you joined our team."

"I heard it's got something to do with magnetism," Barty commented.

"Magnetism? Magnetism, that's the most stupid thing I've heard from you in a long time," replied Billy dismissively.

"Well you explain it so if you're such a genius, Einstein," Barty fired back, feeling a little foolish.

"I can't explain it, nobody can. These woods are just haunted."

"Ah don't tell us that Billy, I'm nervous enough as it is," Cathal pleaded.

"Sure you knew that all along Cathal," replied Billy. "Sure you've heard the story of Seánín Solas and his killer light and all that strange supernatural stuff."

"Yes but I don't believe it anymore."

"You mean, you don't want to believe it anymore," Billy piped back. "That won't make the spirits go away though."

"Ah stop, you're freaking both of us out now," interrupted Barty.

Suddenly Billy hushed the others, holding his index finger to his lips.

"What was that?" he whispered dramatically, pointing into the foggy woods.

"What was what?" Cathal whispered back, with concern

in his voice as he stared into the blankness.

"I'd swear I saw a light coming through the fog."

"Ah don't mind him Cathal," interrupted Barty. "He's winding us up."

"I'm not messing, there's definitely someone or something there. Look, listen…"

Barty and Cathal knew from the tone of his voice that Billy really wasn't messing. The three stood together, looking into the thick fog to see what might be there. Billy and Cathal were by now holding their spades like defensive weapons and Barty, who was standing slightly behind them, was nervously scanning the woods all around him.

"There it is again," exclaimed Billy warily, this time pointing to a faint light a short distance away through the fog.

"I see it too," said Cathal.

"It's Seánín Solas," cried Barty, "let's get out of here."

Before Barty had a chance to run, Billy had grabbed him by the collar of his coat and instructed him to "get down" and "shut up".

The three boys dropped to the ground and watched nervously as the light drew closer.

"Oh, we're finished now," Barty whimpered, his voice trembling.

"Easy Barty, easy," whispered Cathal, trying to calm his friend despite his own fear.

The boys remained motionless but the light kept coming directly towards their position.

"It's coming right for us lads, what should we do?" asked Cathal.

"It's too late to run now," replied Billy with fear in his voice.

The light was now only metres away, and finally it shone directly on the boys' faces, dazzling them as they looked up at it from their "hiding" place on the ground.

Suddenly the beam of light shifted off their faces and on to the face of the being in possession of the light. The boys collectively screamed in terror.

CHAPTER 2
DISCOVERY

"What are you boys screaming at?" protested a soft and feeble voice.

There before the boys stood an old woman, with a wrinkled face and waist length white hair. She was dressed all in black and her appearance was enough to initially frighten the three boys to near delirium, but once she spoke, they were relieved that it was a real person and that she wasn't a ghost or Seánín Solas or anything else!

"Who're you?" asked Billy, rising to his feet and regaining his composure, feeling embarrassed about how he and the others had reacted.

"Why, you're standing in my land," the woman replied sharply, the light now shining on the ground, so that all parties could see each other.

"You're Mrs. Murphy," blurted Barty.

"Yes, who else would I be?"

"We're sorry, Mrs. Murphy," added Cathal. "We thought you were …"

Cathal, through his nervousness, had spoken without thinking, but then stopped mid-sentence and an awkward pause ensued.

"A ghost?" she added sarcastically.

"Um…yeah… sorry."

"Well, for the computer generation, you children sometimes amaze me with your nonsense. Ghosts! Sure there's no such thing."

"We're very sorry Mrs. Murphy," added Billy. "It's just we've heard so many stories about these woods and Seánín Solas and all that."

"And would this be the same Seánín Solas that supposedly haunts these woods with his killer light chasing after trespassers?"

"Am…yeah," replied Barty shyly.

"Well, it obviously wasn't enough to frighten ye to stay out of here in the past, was it?"

The three boys remained silent, their heads bowed. Mrs. Murphy continued and was quite sharp in her tone but spoke with great composure and eloquence.

"Oh, I've heard all the stories over the years about the haunted woods and strange lights. Local gossips with nothing else better to be talking about came up with all of that rubbish! I'll have you know that I personally knew Seánín O'Connor, the man whom you refer to as Seánín Solas. He worked on this estate for decades and was the kindest and gentlest man that ever walked the face of this earth. There was one incident here one night years ago but it had nothing to do with him."

"Was that the man on the barbed wire?" fired Barty spontaneously.

"The man on the barbed wire is what it has become known as, yes. But I'm sure that the version you have heard differs greatly from the real truth. Anyway, enough about that. I came here to ask you boys if you want to come to the house for tea. It is a long standing tradition on this estate that anyone who works here is shown hospitality."

The boys looked at each other, each thinking that it would be rude to refuse the offer, given that it was such a kind gesture. At the same time, they felt uneasy about the old lady, and were equally uncomfortable with the prospect of going into the big old mansion, about which even more ghost stories existed. They really did not have a choice and Billy responded.

"We'd love some tea Mrs. Murphy."

"Well follow me so."

Mrs. Murphy turned and walked in the direction from which she had come, and the boys followed silently behind her through the thick fog. She talked as she walked, giving a brief history of the estate, the woods and the big old house.

"The Murphy Estate was originally the Bradford Estate and consisted of over 8,000 acres of land. It was granted to Major Bentley Bradford of Yorkshire under the Cromwellian settlement of Ireland in the late 1660's. The mansion that I live in today was built by Captain Edward Bradford in the 1770's and was modernised in the 1820's and again in the 1840's. The Murphy family gained possession of the estate in the late 1920's and have lived there since. Sadly, I am the last living member of the Murphy family and I live here all by myself nowadays."

The boys listened with interest as they walked with the lady towards the house, by now having reached a gravel path that led away from the woods.

"During the famine, the estate became a centre for the starving people of the countryside to come to and be fed by

Lady Cecelia Bradford, who ran a soup kitchen in the old stables. It is said that she saved hundreds of local people from starvation through her charity."

"I hope she's still here," blurted Barty, "I'm starving now!"

Billy dug his elbow into his brother's arm but it was too late and the comment had been heard by Mrs. Murphy.

"And what age would you think she'd be young man if she were still here now?"

"Am…old?" responded Barty after some hesitation.

"Yes, she would be wouldn't she? You're not very bright it seems," quipped Mrs. Murphy, as Billy and Cathal fought back laughter.

"You can't see it now, but the walled garden is just over there to our left and in front of you in a few moments you should be able to see the lights of the house."

The boys scanned their surroundings, all the while following the old lady with the light. Sure enough, after a few seconds, a dim light could be seen through the fog and, as they drew closer, the outline of an enormous house became clear. In the available light, the boys could see that the house was indeed a mansion, consisting of three floors, countless big old windows, with four great square towers rising at each corner of the building and a front facing gable reaching far above the magnificent main entrance, which was supported by four round pillars. Numerous chimneys emerged at various locations from the roof and most of the walls were covered with a thick coating of ivy. The house was partially surrounded to the sides and rear by a line of tall ash trees, their branches bare of leaves given the time of year. The rooms in the two upstairs floors were all in darkness but a light was on in the ground floor room just to the left of the entrance.

"Wow, it's unreal!" gasped Cathal with excitement upon seeing the building.

"I can assure you that it's very real!" responded Mrs. Murphy, as she led the boys through the gravel yard and up five or six stone steps to the front door. With some effort, she pushed the stiff and heavy door open, the hinges creaking loudly and unnervingly as it moved. The boys could see a huge entrance hallway of black and white floor tiles and a great oak staircase with a thick red carpet draping the steps. The white plastered walls looked to measure at least four metres from floor to ceiling and were adorned with huge old canvass portraits of various individuals, whom the boys assumed were former residents of the mansion.

"Do come in, but leave your boots at the door," she instructed.

Instantly, the boys noticed the strange smell of the old house and its many antique furnishing as they duly removed their wellingtons, which were quite muddy after their day on the plantation. Cathal quietly chuckled to himself upon seeing Barty's big toe sticking completely out through a rather sizable hole in one of his socks, but didn't want to embarrass him by passing any remark.

"Now, follow me."

Mrs. Murphy led the boys past the bottom of the staircase into a room on their left hand side, where the lights had been left on. Along the way, as he passed by, Cathal felt a cold draft coming down the stairs from above and noticed that, rather unusually, a large wooden sideboard sat right across the top step of the stairs, effectively making it impossible to access the upper floors.

"This is the drawing room," Mrs. Murphy informed the trio. You'll be seated here while I prepare the tea and phone your grandfather to collect you."

The boys sat down on an antique couch as Mrs. Murphy left the room, pulling the door closed in her wake, the dark wooden floorboards creaking underfoot as she left. The trio were comfortably warm, thanks mainly to the large coal fire that burned in the beautiful wooden fireplace, which was the central feature in the room, and was just a short distance from the couch. The walls were decorated with beige floral wallpaper and like the hallway, supported many portraits and landscape paintings in bulky golden coloured frames. Over the fireplace, a large stuffed stag head hung from the wall, its long antlers stretching almost as wide as the chimney breast, while its eyes seemed to be monitoring the three occupiers of the couch beneath.

"This place is so creepy," whispered Barty to Cathal, who was seated between the Shanahan brothers.

"I know, but it's kind of cool too though, don't you think?" replied Cathal, his head twisting in all directions to take in all that he could see.

"Look, that fella in that painting there looks the spit of Luis Suarez!" remarked Barty, pointing to one of the portraits, as the boys laughed.

"This place is class," said Billy joining the conversation, as he rose to his feet and darted to a corner of the room, his attention captured by a suit of knight armour that stood there.

"This is mad," he exclaimed, as he studied the armour up close, the entire suit standing as if a knight still occupied it.

"Look, it's even got a sword and shield and everything. I wonder if the eye guard still works?"

"Don't touch it Billy," Cathal whispered anxiously, fearful of doing any damage to what was obviously a very valuable piece of historical artefact.

Cathal's words were in vain and Billy proceeded to fiddle with the armour, moving the eye guard up and down before turning his attention to the arms, which he also started to move. He probably would have stopped due to Cathal's protestations, but Barty found his brother's puppetry hilarious and encouraged him to continue. Billy was behind the armour suit and had the "knight" waving at Barty when Mrs. Murphy opened the door and saw what was happening.

"Come away from that you idiot, that's a very valuable antique!" she bellowed at Billy, who quickly stopped what he was doing and returned to the couch, where Barty and Cathal were awkwardly staring straight ahead at the fireplace. "Didn't you ever learn to respect other people's property?"

"Sorry Mrs. Murphy," replied Billy, his head bowed.

"You boys can't be left alone for one minute! I've a good mind not to give you any tea and cake."

"Ah please Mrs. Murphy, I'm starvin' altogether!" reacted Barty instantly, the mention of cake drawing an instinctive retort from him.

"Have your manners young man. You're not at home now. You don't deserve it and I'm a bigger fool for inviting you in here."

The three boys sat silently on the couch and after a moment, the old lady realised that perhaps she had over reacted to what had just happened.

"This is the last chance I'll give you three," she said in a more conciliatory tone. "Don't budge from that couch while I go to the kitchen."

With that she left the room again.

"Sorry lads," whispered Billy, by now smirking at what had just happened.

"You're some ape!" Cathal replied. "That's probably worth more than the whole estate all by itself, and there you were pretending it's a toy."

"Ah lighten up Sir Moansalot, sure didn't Barty enjoy it."

"Who's almost worse to be laughing at you," remarked Cathal.

"Poor Barty can't help it, he's just easily amused," observed Billy.

"Excuse me, stop talking about me, I'm sitting right here!" protested Barty. "Anyway, if it wasn't for me, ye'd be out the door with no cake."

"We haven't got the cake yet, so don't count your chickens," exclaimed Cathal.

"Ssh, listen! What's that?" interrupted Billy suddenly.

"What's what?" replied Barty dismissively.

"Shut up and you might hear it," whispered Billy forcefully.

The three listened as the faint sound of beautiful music could be heard.

"Do ye hear that? It's a flute," exclaimed Billy.

"What's she doing playing the flute, I thought she was making the tea?" remarked Barty, confused.

"It's probably just the radio lads," added Cathal. "Listen again."

The three sat silently again and they could clearly hear the music and this time it seemed even louder.

"I'd swear it's coming from upstairs," whispered Billy.

"Maybe she left the radio or TV on up there," suggested Barty.

"I doubt it lads," added Cathal. "It looked to me on the way in that the upstairs part of the house hasn't been used for years."

"That music is definitely coming from upstairs and no way is a radio or TV that clear," observed Billy.

"Maybe there's another way up there other than the main staircase?" suggested Barty.

"Maybe, but why would she go up there playing the flute when she's gone getting the tea?" mused Billy. "Unless there's someone else in the house?"

"But why would she have lied about being here all alone Billy?" asked Cathal.

"I don't know, maybe she's just daft?"

Just then the music stopped and a few seconds later, the door opened and Mrs. Murphy returned, carrying a tray of tea and cakes for the boys. All three of the boys thanked Mrs. Murphy for going to the trouble of preparing the refreshments but inwardly, they were trying to figure out the mysterious music, and thought it just a little strange that it stopped just seconds before she re-entered the room.

The tea and cakes were rapidly devoured by the three hungry forestry workers. During further small talk with Mrs. Murphy, the conversation strayed to the resemblance of the man in the painting to Luis Suarez, whom Mrs. Murphy had never heard of. Barty immediately felt foolish for bringing the subject up, and especially for approaching the subject by asking Mrs. Murphy if she was a Liverpool supporter. Thankfully for him, the conversation was cut short when Granda's noisy old car could be heard arriving in the yard of the mansion.

"Well boys, it was nice getting to know you a little better. I suppose you're not as bad as I had initially thought," declared Mrs. Murphy bluntly, as she rose to her feet.

"We'll take that as a compliment," replied Billy roguishly.

"Thank you very much for your hospitality Mrs. Murphy and for your kindness about everything that's happened," said Cathal.

"That's alright. You're forgiven. Just don't do it again or I will have you sent away to prison!"

The boys smiled in awkward appreciation.

"Oh by the way," said Barty, "you're a beautiful musician Mrs. Murphy."

"A beautiful what?" she replied, clearly confused by his comment.

"Wasn't that you playing the flute earlier?"

"No boy, it was not me," she replied with a serious demeanour.

"Ah, so it was the radio or TV after all?"

"I haven't had the radio or television on since morning."

"Oh you have other visitors so?"

"No, I'm here all by myself," she explained, a worried look coming to her face.

"Okay, we better not be keeping Cathal's granda waiting,"

exclaimed Billy, changing the subject and grabbing Barty's arm to pull him towards the door. Barty was still thinking aloud as he was putting his boots back on at the doorway, but Cathal and Billy kept making enough small talk to avoid any further awkwardness.

"Bye Mrs. Murphy and thanks again," cried Cathal, as the boys departed hastily, pulling the big wooden door firmly shut in their wake.

"You're some eejit Barty!" muttered Billy under his breath as they walked away from the door.

"What did I say?"

"You should have kept your mouth shut about the music, you'll frighten the life out of the poor woman."

The boys sat into Granda's car, which was ticking over in the yard, surrounded by a thick cloud of smoke.

"How was yer day?" Granda asked. "Hope ye didn't see any ghosts in the big house!"

"No, we didn't see anything strange," replied Cathal. "But we did hear something very strange!"

CHAPTER 3
A STORY FOR THE ROAD

"So ye heard something very strange? That's interesting!" Granda remarked calmly but solemnly as he drove slowly along the winding gravel driveway that lead away from Murphy's Estate towards the main Killcrown to Ballycastle road.

"We did Granda and I'm very confused," replied Cathal.

"Ya Mick, either Mrs. Murphy was pulling a fast one on us, or there's something really odd going on in that house," added Billy with excitement in his voice.

The three boys proceeded to tell Granda the whole story in detail about the sound of the beautiful music from upstairs in the mansion. Granda listened to every word intently without saying a thing. When all three boys had said everything they needed to say, Granda pulled over to the side of the road. He switched on the interior light and turned to face Cathal, who was sitting in the front passenger seat, and the Shanahan brothers, who were seated in the rear seat but were now leaning forward to hear what Granda was about to say. From the look on his face, before he spoke a word, the boys knew that he was going to say something very important.

"Boys, I think ye have just heard a ghost." Granda declared to a collective gasp from the three passengers. "I think I should explain the whole story to ye, and ye can make up yer own minds after that."

Granda began.

"It was 1921 and the country was in turmoil in the midst of the War of Independence. The Black and Tans had been sent over here from Britain to try to crush the Irish rebels, who were fighting to secure our freedom. The Black and Tans were a terrible bunch, and terrorised the Irish countryside, burning people out of their homes and doing all sorts of unspeakable things to the poor Irish. Ballycastle and Killcrown didn't escape their terror and were very troubled areas at the time. Both places were known to be rebel strongholds, and so the Black and Tans were never far away.

Anyway, in the middle of all of this chaos, a young rebel from Ballycastle, by the name of Micheál MacDiarmada, fell in love with a young lady who lived in the big house where Mrs. Murphy lives now. Her name was Lady Evelyn Bradford, and she was the daughter of the local Magistrate, Lord Henry Bradford. Now, it was bad enough that a young Catholic lad from the area should fall in love with one of the Protestant upper class, but the fact that young Micheál was a rebel made matters much worse. When Lord Henry heard of the romance, he immediately forbade his daughter from seeing Micheál, and on top of that, he issued a warrant for Micheál's arrest for being a traitor to the crown.

The young couple were devastated, but they weren't going to let Lord Henry and his outdated views come between them. They continued seeing each other, in secret, usually at night time when she would sneak out of the house and into the woods. Sometimes, he would even sneak into the big old house by climbing up the ivy to Lady Evelyn's bedroom window. This was very risky business of course, but Micheál was a bit of a daredevil and got great excitement out of sneaking into the mansion. This went on for a few months without anybody ever knowing. Some nights, Lady Evelyn would even take her little boat and row across to the Ballycastle side of the river to meet her sweetheart outside of the confines of the estate. They were deeply in love and planned to elope and marry as soon as the War of Independence was over.

Then, one night, Micheál was coming to see Lady Evelyn in her room, as he had done many times before. It was a rainy night as he made his way across the River Clane and through the woods to the lawn of the mansion. He covertly made his way to the side of the house and began climbing up the ivy towards the bedroom window above. After all the rain, the ivy had become a bit slippery and maybe poor old Micheál had grown a bit careless during all the times he had climbed up there. As he approached the window, his foot slipped from the ivy and Micheál fell all the way down to the ground, banging the back of his head as he landed.

Lord Henry heard the commotion from his chambers and called his security guards, who quickly captured the dazed young rebel as he was still lying on the ground. Despite him needing urgent medical attention, they took him down to the cellar beneath the mansion and sent for the Black and Tans, who were stationed in nearby Killcrown.

During all of this, poor Lady Evelyn was deeply distraught in her bedroom, and had been locked in by her father so she couldn't interfere with proceedings. She knew that the security guards had taken Micheál to the cellar, and not being able to climb out of her window to see her sweetheart, she decided she would communicate with him in another way.

Micheál was in the cellar tied to a chair, still a bit dazed after his fall but was starting to come around. He was anxiously pondering what lay ahead when, as if it were a dream, he heard the sound of the sweetest music coming from upstairs in the mansion. Lady Evelyn was a talented flutist, and so she played music to soothe Micheál throughout that dreadful night. Servants who worked in the house at the time later said that she hardly stopped all night, constantly playing tune after tune for her injured hero in the cellar.

As morning neared, the rumble of engines could be heard approaching from the distance, and before long, two lorries full of heavily armed Black and Tans pulled into the yard of the mansion. They quickly took the injured prisoner from the cellar and bundled him into the back of one of the lorries. Poor Evelyn was screaming from her bedroom window as they took Micheál away, with one of the brutes even butting him with his rifle when he tried to wave goodbye to her. The lorries sped away from the yard and poor Evelyn was heartbroken.

I'd like to tell ye that the local rebels came to the rescue of young Micheál, but if I did I'd be telling a lie. The truth is that none of his friends knew that he had gone to see Lady Evelyn that night, so nobody knew that he had been taken prisoner."

"What happened to him Granda?" asked Cathal, he and the Shanahans captivated by the story.

"Private Micheál MacDiarmada was murdered by the Black and Tans and buried somewhere in Murphy's Woods, never to be seen again."

"That's awful," gasped Barty. "Where did they bury him?"

"Well, that's the thing," said Granda. "Nobody knows where exactly."

"Did they ever get the Black and Tans for what they did Mick?" asked Billy.

"Oh they did for sure lads. Of the twenty two Black and Tans that came to take Micheál away that morning, not one made it back to England alive. The entire lot of them were all hunted down one by one by Micheál's comrades, and they all met their maker before that year was over."

"And what about poor Lady Evelyn?" asked Barty.

"Well," said Granda, "I wish I had a happier ending for her too, but it wasn't to be. Lady Evelyn never spoke another word and never left her bedroom again, alive at least. Despite all of the efforts of her family and their doctors, she became a complete recluse. Night after night she would stand by her window playing her flute for her beloved Micheál. Then one night, the music stopped. When her mother went to check on her, she found her dead in her bed, her flute in one hand and an engagement ring, presumably from Micheál, in the other. The doctors concluded that she had died from a broken heart."

"That's really sad Granda. But, what's the story with the music that we heard?"

"Well, as I said, one night the music stopped. The reason: poor Lady Evelyn had died. In her diary, which she kept beside her bed, she had written that she wished to be buried with her sweetheart, Micheál. Of course, her father, Lord Henry, deemed that this would be out of the question completely, and so the location of Micheál's grave remained a secret. Contrary to her wishes, they had Lady Evelyn's remains buried alone in the church yard in Killcrown, far away from poor Micheál, who is still buried somewhere under Murphy's Woods to this very night."

"So what about the music?" quizzed Billy a little impatiently.

"Well, the very night after Lady Evelyn was laid to her so-called rest, the family were sitting in the dining room for dinner when they heard someone upstairs playing the flute. At first they thought it was someone connected to Micheál and the rebels trying to play mind games with the family for what had been done to Micheál. They sent for their security guards, but no intruder could be found, even though they searched every inch of the mansion and the gardens. The following night, the music started again, and like the previous night, nobody or nothing could be found. The music continued every single night until eventually, after a few months, the Bradfords and all of their servants and staff moved out of the house and moved away to England. Officially, they said they moved because of threats from the rebels, but in reality, it was the hauntings by Lady Evelyn that frightened them away."

"That's amazing Granda," remarked Cathal. "But, did the hauntings not stop once Lady Evelyn had got revenge on her family for what they had done?"

"No. Over the years, many people have heard the music. The strange thing is that some people hear it and some don't."

"You mean, if two people are in the house at the same time in the same place, you're saying one might hear it and one might not?" asked Billy.

"Exactly," replied Granda. "I can't explain it. It's just supernatural. And, by the way, I have two theories on why I think Lady Evelyn's music can still be heard."

"Oh tell us," Barty gasped with curiosity.

"Well, firstly, Cathal, you just assumed that Lady Evelyn was seeking revenge on her family by haunting them, and that's a possibility, but my view is that if that was the case, the music would have stopped when they left the mansion. It didn't, which leads me to believe that her ghost still plays the music for two reasons. One, her dying request to be buried with her sweetheart was not honoured, and her spirit is not at rest. And two, she is still playing music to her sweetheart Micheál."

"But isn't he buried inside in the woods?" asked a confused Barty.

"Yes he is," replied Granda, "but, here's the thing. Over the years, a number of people have also reported seeing the outline of a young man in the cellar of the house, at the exact place where Micheál MacDiarmada was held prisoner in the hours before he was murdered by the Black and Tans!"

All three boys gasped in disbelief at this latest revelation.

"Oh my God, that's so sad," exclaimed Cathal. "Poor Micheál isn't at rest either."

"I'm never going back there, that's for sure," added Barty.

"So," observed Billy with a slightly sceptical tone, "Lady Evelyn is haunting the house and Micheál MacDiarmada is haunting the cellar, and just for good measure, our old friend Seánín Solas is haunting the woods. That makes three ghosts Mick?"

"At least," confirmed Granda. "And do ye know what else, Cathal, you're a direct descendent of Micheál MacDiaramada, his sister having married your great-great-grandfather, making him your great-great granduncle. Sure there's even a monument in his honour just outside Ballycastle Village."

Granda turned off the interior light and started driving on the road towards home again.

"Murphy's Estate is one of the most haunted places in Kerry, if not Ireland. Some people believe it, some people don't and some people just don't want to admit that they believe it, but in my opinion, if you could hear the music, you're a believer."

Not many words were spoken on the remainder of the fifteen minute journey home, with all four occupants of the car contemplating the discussion that had just taken place. Granda dropped the Shanahans off at their house and proceeded home with Cathal, where the pair enjoyed a big plate of bacon, cabbage and potatoes before Cathal slipped away to bed around 10pm. Exhausted after his busy day of hard labour and tales of the supernatural, he drifted away to sleep listening to the winter rain pelt against his window, thinking about his murdered great-great granduncle lying somewhere in an unmarked grave under the soil of Murphy's Woods.

Granda's Cottage

CHAPTER 4
A BIG DAY OUT

It was Saturday, October 12th, and the mid-morning sunshine illuminated Cathal's room through the closed curtains.

"Come on Cathal, we'll be leaving soon," he heard a familiar voice call from downstairs.

Then, remembering the day that it was, Cathal jumped out of bed and was dressed and in the kitchen in minutes. He devoured his breakfast and was sitting in the back seat of the car before anyone else. Cathal loved gaelic football and today, his local club were playing in the provincial semi-final, and he would be there to cheer them on. The journey would take about two hours, but Cathal had prepared well for it, bringing his iPod and plenty of games, something his three travelling companions weren't too pleased about. They would have preferred his undivided company for the journey.

Hundreds of supporters from Cathal's town made the same journey that day, most of them proudly wearing their club colours. As it turned out, Cathal put his iPod and games aside about a half an hour into the journey and realised that it was far more enjoyable to talk to and listen to the people that were travelling with him.

The match was a dogged affair and Cathal was sure that his club were going to lose and be knocked out of the championship until a last minute goal clutched victory from the jaws of defeat. It was the greatest moment in his life to date as a football supporter. Ecstatic after the win, Cathal and his companions embarked on the journey back home, discussing every detail of the sporting contest before stopping at their favourite pizza parlour for a delicious meal. Cathal always felt that the best food is the food on the way home from a football match, especially if his team had just won.

On the rest of the journey home, all four discussed the great victory all over again.

"Cathal, you'll be late," a man's voice called.

"What do you mean Dad?" Cathal replied.

"Cathal, you'll be late for Mass?"

"What?"

Cathal could see Granda standing at his bedroom door. There was no sign of his father, mother or his brother and he wasn't in the back seat of the family car, but in his new bedroom at Granda's cottage. It was Sunday, December 15th and it was time to get up for Mass.

CHAPTER 5
MASS

Cathal never liked Mass. He always found it very boring. He and Granda arrived at the chapel just as 10am Mass was about to start, passing Billy and Barty Shanahan in the entrance porch as they made their way in. The Shanahans were continuing a long standing tradition in Ballycastle (standing being the operative word), where many of the men of the parish would stand in the little porch inside the main chapel door, or even rest against the wall outside the door, instead of actually taking one of the many vacant seats inside the building itself. Cathal thought it the strangest thing he had ever seen and wondered why someone would go to the trouble of going to Mass at all, if they were just going to stand outside the door.

After what felt like an eternity for Cathal, but was only about forty five minutes in reality, Fr. O'Rourke, the elderly parish priest, announced that Mass was almost ended, except for some local announcements.

"My dear people, just a few announcements before we go:

Firstly, next Saturday night, December 21st, St. Joseph's National School will hold the Christmas Nativity Play and Concert in aid of the church roof fund, to be held in the parish hall, beginning at 8 o'clock. Your support for this would be greatly appreciated.

Also, it would be remiss of me here this morning not to refer to the events of the last week here in Ballycastle, which saw us become the centre of local, national and international news. In fact, a friend of mine in the missions in Tanzania phoned me during the week after seeing Ballycastle on the evening news over there."

A few members of the congregation chuckled at the thought of some priest over in Tanzania seeing Ballycastle on his TV, some amazed that they even had televisions in whatever country he had just mentioned. Meanwhile Billy and Barty Shanahan slowly shuffled their way in from the porch, to the rear of the church, to a position from where they would be able to better absorb the praise that they anticipated from the priest. Cathal sat upright in his seat, for once paying total attention to the cleric's every word. Fr. O'Rourke continued:

"When God was handing out courage and bravery, we can all be very proud that he didn't pass this little community by. In fact, he gave us more than our fair share. That fair share was put to good use last Saturday night and Sunday morning and I want to acknowledge these great gifts here this morning."

The three boys were bursting with excitement, ready for their moment of glory. Fr. O'Rourke continued:

"People of Ballycastle, please put your hands together and give a hearty round of applause in appreciation of the one and only, PEGGY MOORE!"

The church erupted into a rapturous round of applause, cheering and wolf whistles, as Peggy Moore, a large framed widow in her mid-sixties, seated at the very front row of seats, rose to her feet, turned to the congregation, waved liked the queen and bowed like a theatre performer, absorbing every ounce of attention like a sponge would soak water. The boys were disgusted. Their moment of glory and recognition had been misappropriated to the very person they disliked most in Ballycastle – Peggy Moore – "the nosiest, gossipiest and pettiest auld bag of them all" as Billy would call her!

The Shanahan brothers could take no more of it and stormed out the chapel door, feeling robbed, Billy remarking to Barty that Peggy's bows made her look like the fat lady after she'd finished singing. Cathal, with no direct escape route, had to sit where he was and endure the entire adulation of Peggy, although he felt somewhat consoled by a recognising pat on the knee from Granda, who sensed his grandson's disappointment. When calm was restored in the church, Peggy resumed her seat and Fr. O'Rourke sent everyone on their blessed way.

As Cathal was slowly progressing through the crowded aisle towards the doorway, he was met by his other least favourite person in Ballycastle, his veteran school teacher, Master Seán Ó Luing.

"Ah, Cathal, there you are," remarked The Master, in his usual snipe like tone.

"Good morning Master," replied Cathal shyly, privately noticing that The Master was wearing the exact same shabby old grey suit that he wore every day of the week in the classroom, with his overall appearance as dishevelled as ever.

"I was thinking that you and the Shanahans will play the three wise men in the nativity play next Saturday night," remarked The Master, stroking the grey hair of his bearded chin between the thumb and index finger of his right hand.

"That's grand Master, we would love to," replied Cathal.

"No, I'm not asking you, I'm telling you, although the name "wise" men is a bit ironic, given the three lads we're dealing with. Now, you tell the other two and let there be no complaining."

"What a horrible man," Cathal thought to himself.

"Oh, and we need a donkey too, so bring your grandfather's one to school on Friday for the dress rehearsal and on Saturday night for the real thing."

The Master turned and walked away without even bidding farewell, as Cathal was left to ponder the potential for embarrassment with the involvement of Paddy, his grandfather's donkey, in the concert.

"Paddy is too old to perform basic functions, never mind perform for an audience," he contemplated with a sigh.

Outside in the church yard, as Granda chatted with some of the locals, Cathal noticed that the Shanahan brothers were waiting for him by the church gate.

"Well, that was an anti-climax!" remarked Cathal as he approached the pair, a clear look of disappointment still etched on their faces.

"Anti-climax? More like the anti-Christ when I saw that one getting all the praise!" complained Billy.

"It's typical Ballycastle," moaned Barty. "Just because it was us, the good for nothing Shanahans, they find someone else to heap the praise on."

"Sure look lads, we know ourselves what we achieved, isn't that all that matters?" posed Cathal, somewhat philosophically.

"No, that is not all that matters," responded Billy with great conviction in his voice. "It's no good if you're not recognised by your peers."

"That's rubbish Billy," Cathal said in disagreement.

"Ok so," argued Billy. "Take Usain Bolt, the fastest man on two feet. Do you think he'd be happy to do his thing behind closed doors where only he would know that he is faster than any man ever? No. So why should I be content if I achieve something and someone else gets the praise for it?

"Well I see your point but the point I'm making is, who cares what a few old biddies around here are saying? Everyone knows deep down that our actions saved the day last weekend," argued Cathal.

"Hang on lads, I've got a question," interrupted Barty.

The others paused, Cathal expecting a philosophical contribution to the discussion, Billy, knowing him better, predicting what actually transpired.

"Who's Usain Bolt?"

"I knew you were going to ask that question!" sighed Billy, as Barty pretended to have been only joking, although he really wasn't.

"What are ye doing for the rest of the day lads?" asked Cathal, moving to a different subject intentionally.

"Well, I actually have to go back over to Murphy's Woods," explained Barty. "I left my back sack there yesterday evening and I need it for school in the morning."

"Well that wasn't very clever was it Barty?" observed Billy harshly.

"You'd swear I meant to," responded Barty defensively. "It was your fault we had to go there in the first place, and my back sack was the last thing I thought of when that fog came in over us so quickly."

"Do you want me to come with you Barty?" offered Cathal.

"I'd rather not go alone. That place is so creepy."

"I'll be with you so. What about you Billy, you coming too?"

"Well I suppose I better to try to keep you two out of trouble," responded Billy.

"Will we take the boat across the river as usual?" asked Cathal.

"Yep, our mother is working and we couldn't be looking for a drive from your Granda again after yesterday," said Barty.

"Perfect," said Cathal. "Meet ye at the usual spot at the bottom of the road at two?"

The boys agreed their plan and parted company. In the afternoon, they would be heading back to Murphy's Woods.

Where some of the action takes place...

CHAPTER 6
BACK ON THE WATER

Granda's routine every Sunday was:

9am – Eat breakfast.

10am – Go to Mass.

11am - Buy the paper at Ted Hanratty's shop.

11.05am to 12pm - Chat with Ted about everything from the situation in the Middle East to the county football championship.

12 noon - Go to McCarthy's Bar for lunch and a few glasses of porter.

6pm – Watch the news in McCarthy's Lounge while enjoying a supper of a toasted ham and cheese sandwich with chips.

7pm – 9pm - Read whatever part of the newspaper that wasn't already read during the afternoon.

9pm - Watch the news again.

9.30pm – Have one for the road.

10pm – Return home and go to bed.

It was a fairly rigid routine, which only ever changed if there was a major event taking place, such as a local funeral (which delayed the post Mass itinerary by about a half an hour for the rest of the day), a major football match (which Granda might go to if he got a drive from someone), or, as was the case recently, if Granda had important business to carry out, like the day he collected Cathal to bring him to his new home in Ballycastle. Other than those reasons though, you could be pretty sure where to find Mick Kavanagh on any given Sunday.

Therefore, it was no great surprise to Cathal, after he and Granda had enjoyed lunch in McCarthy's Bar, that the old man told him that he was free to have the afternoon to himself, a nice way of saying, "leave me have my space!" Of course, this suited Cathal perfectly, as it allowed him to meet the Shanahan brothers as had been agreed.

As the trio made their way to Ballycastle Pier, from where they would take their little wooden rowing boat across the River Clane, they remarked on how relaxing it was to be able to stroll along the road in the broad daylight and not worry about being seen by anybody, unlike their previous excursions along that same route. Along the way, Cathal remarked about how he couldn't stop thinking about the "ghost music" that they had heard the previous evening, and all three of the boys agreed that the story of Lady Evelyn and Micheál MacDiarmada was an utter tragedy.

It took only a few minutes to cross the 100 metre stretch of calm, slow-moving water that separated Ballycastle Slipway from Killcrown Slipway, and soon the boys were making their way towards Murphy's Woods.

Along the way to the entrance of the woods, the boys encountered a number of local people, all out for Sunday walks, enjoying the unseasonably mild and sunny weather conditions. The road from the town of Killcrown to Killcrown Pier was a popular recreational route, as it was rarely used by motorised traffic. The boys greeted the people that they met along the way, and received friendly Kerry salutes in return.

A group of three middle-aged women from Killcrown passed them by at the point where the boys entered Murphy's Woods through a breach in the perimeter fence. The women recognised the boys and the boys smiled back at them. After a few moments of walking through the woodland, the boys reached the clearing where they had been planting trees on the previous day. Barty located his back sack without difficulty and before they knew it, the friends were heading back home, leaving Murphy's Woods through the fence where they entered, following the road to Killcrown Pier, rowing back across to Ballycastle Pier and walking back to their respective homes. Unlike the outward journey, they met nobody on the way home. Cathal parted company with the Shanahans at their house just after 4pm, and was back to Granda's little cottage at the foot of the hill just before the dark. He lit the fire and sat down to finish his weekend school homework, and had his books packed away by 6pm. He made his supper and ate it while he watched television. Cathal went to bed just after 9pm, and Granda returned home at his usual time of 10pm.

St. Joseph's National School

CHAPTER 7
PRIME SUSPECTS

The Master was in the middle of giving an unnecessarily complicated account of the first lunar landing when a knock came to the classroom door, forcing him to leave the room for a few moments. The students of 3rd, 4th, 5th and 6th classes all breathed a collective sigh of relief when the lesson was interrupted, after The Master somehow made one of mankind's greatest achievements seem boring. Somehow, he had managed to turn one giant leap for mankind into one giant monotonous Monday morning lecture. Moments later, the students breathed sighs of amazement, when The Master returned to the classroom accompanied by the local Garda, Jim O'Sullivan, who had a serious look on his face. All of the students wondered what the reason was for his visit.

The Garda scanned the classroom with his eyes, eventually making and holding eye contact with Cathal, whose initial reaction was to nod back at the Garda in a gesture of salutation, the pair having been acquainted due to the events of recent times. However, the Garda did not return the salute. Instead, he spoke sternly.

"Cathal Kavanagh, I would like to speak to you outside please," said Garda Jim, the whole classroom muttering in surprise upon hearing the words.

Garda Jim left the classroom and Cathal rose to his feet and followed him, his heart racing with fearful curiosity. As he passed The Master at the classroom door, Cathal received a venomous stare that said much without any words having to be uttered. When he reached the corridor, Cathal noticed that Garda Jim had proceeded to The Master's office, where he stood at the door and called Cathal to come "in here".

As Cathal walked the short distance along the corridor, worries rushed through his mind about why the local policeman wanted to speak with him. Bad memories flooded back to Cathal. The last time a Garda came to visit him was the morning on which he was told that his parents and brother had died tragically. That horrible event was something that Cathal had almost completely blocked from his memory, but now the circumstances reopened a closed door. His fears turned to his only living relative. He wondered if something bad had happened to Granda, if he had been involved in some sort of accident or some other type of trouble. He braced himself for bad news, but was momentarily relieved to see Granda sitting in The Master's office waiting for him when he walked through the door.

"What's going on Granda?" Cathal gasped, but Granda did not engage with him. Instead, he looked away when Cathal spoke to him, an angry look etched across his face, his body language defensive and distant.

"Sit down Cathal," instructed Garda Jim, before continuing to speak, remaining in a standing position.

"Cathal, I have reason to believe that you were involved in a criminal incident yesterday. Have you anything to say?"

Cathal was shocked by the statement and for a moment, could not even recall what had happened on the previous day, such was his state of surprise. He looked to Granda, who was staring back at him, expressionless.

"Well, are you going to answer me? Where were you yesterday?" pressed the Garda.

Cathal gathered his senses after a few moments of confusion and then remembered the sequence of his activities from the previous day.

"Well, I went to Mass. Then I had lunch with Granda in McCarthy's. After that, I met the Shanahans and we went to Murphy's Woods. We came home. I did my homework, watched telly and went to bed around 9pm. That was it."

"Went to Murphy's Woods? What time was that at?" asked the Garda.

"I'm not sure exactly, about half two or three maybe."

"What were ye doing there?"

"Barty forgot his school bag there on Saturday when we were replanting the trees and we went back to get it."

"That was convenient," remarked the Garda, slyly. "Did ye go anywhere else on the estate other than the woods?"

"No."

"What time did ye leave the woods?"

"Straight away."

"Did ye meet anyone?"

"On the way there, yes, we met a lot of walkers, but I don't recall meeting anybody on the way home."

"Why was that?"

"I don't know, we just didn't meet anyone!"

"So, as I understand it, a lot of people saw ye going in

there, but nobody saw ye coming home. Is that because it was dark by the time ye were finished what ye were doing?"

"No, we left straight away once we got Barty's bag back! It was still bright when I got back to Granda's!"

"Was your grandfather at home when you got home?"

"No."

"When did he see you after that?"

"This morning."

"Why didn't he see you last night?"

"Because I was in bed when he came home."

"In bed. Are you sure you were in bed?"

"Yes."

"What time did you go to bed?"

"About 9pm."

"So you're telling me that nobody saw you and you saw nobody from the time ye went into Murphy's Estate yesterday until you got up for school this morning?"

"Ah, yes, I suppose."

"You suppose?"

"Yes. I mean no, I don't suppose. I didn't see anybody. Why so anyway? What's this all about? Look, if it's about trespassing, I know that technically we were trespassing when we went in to get Barty's bag back, but I didn't think it would be this much of a problem since we had permission to be there all day Saturday."

"This is a lot more serious than trespassing Cathal. This is a burglary investigation and you and the Shanahan brothers could be in serious trouble!"

"How on earth could it be burglary, sure we didn't steal anything?"

"Cathal, I am going to have to ask you to come to the Garda Station with us. Your grandfather will accompany you. I'm going to get to the bottom of this."

Cathal, Granda and Garda Jim left The Master's office and went straight out to the school yard, Cathal not even being given the opportunity to retrieve his school bag and coat from the classroom. The first things Cathal saw when he walked out to the school yard were two Garda patrol cars parked in waiting at the school gates. One of them was just driving away as he approached and Cathal caught a glimpse of Billy and Barty Shanahan sitting in the rear seat, accompanied by their mother, who appeared far from pleased. Garda Jim put Cathal and Granda sitting in the rear seat of the second car and drove them to Killcrown Garda station, which was about fifteen minutes away.

Upon arriving at Killcrown Station, Cathal and Granda were led to a small, cold and plain walled interview room, lit by a white fluorescent tube that buzzed loudly and dimmed slightly every minute or so. They were seated side by side at a long table, which sat between them and the door. One grey plastic chair lay vacant on the side of the table nearer the door. When Cathal and Granda were seated, Garda Jim left the room. Once they were alone, Cathal immediately protested his innocence to Granda, but the old man was having none of it and simply ignored his grandson. After a while, Cathal gave up trying to talk to Granda and decided to wait for whatever would happen next. Inside, he was afraid and worried, but on top of all of this, he was deeply disappointed that Granda would think so little of him as to judge him guilty without even hearing his side of the story. Then he thought of all of the shenanigans that he and the Shanahans had gotten up to since Cathal had arrived in Ballycastle, and considered that Granda probably had good reason to be doubtful or even suspicious. Still, he felt let down by Granda's total blanking of him.

After about fifteen minutes of anxiously waiting in silence, a man wearing ordinary civilian clothing entered the room and sat down in the vacant seat. A tall and thin man, aged about forty, with a shaved head, he spoke with a strong Cork accent when he introduced himself as Detective TJ O'Grady.

"Mick Kavanagh, isn't it?" he asked Granda, shaking his hand as the old man nodded in agreement.

"And you are Cathal Kavanagh?"

"Yes," confirmed Cathal, shaking the detective's hand.

"And Mick, you are Cathal's legal guardian?"

"Yes, I am."

"Okay, just to inform you that this conversation is being recorded and you have the right to have a solicitor present, should you so wish."

"Don't mind those solicitors," replied Granda, dismissively. "And even if I wanted one, I couldn't afford one."

"Okay," said the detective. "Let's proceed."

He fixed his eyes firmly on Cathal.

"Well Cathal, you seem to be in big trouble. Is there anything you want to tell me?"

"Yes," replied Cathal.

Granda sat up in his chair. Cathal continued.

"I want to know what on earth is going on here? I've done nothing wrong!"

"I'll stop you there Cathal," interrupted Detective O'Grady. "You see, the Shanahan brothers have already told us everything, and it doesn't sound too good for you, so you'd be better off giving us your end of the story and the judge might go a bit easier on you when you go to court."

"But they couldn't have told you anything 'cause there just isn't anything to tell!"

"Look boy, just tell the truth," interrupted Granda angrily, his first time speaking to Cathal since meeting him in The Master's office.

"But I didn't do anything wrong," protested Cathal.

"Look Cathal, I'll cut you a deal," offered Detective O'Grady. "Sometime between 3pm yesterday afternoon and 11pm last night, someone or some group broke into the mansion on Murphy's Estate and stole some very valuable items. Amongst the items stolen was a valuable painting and a highly valuable old armour suit, the same suit of armour that you and the Shanahan brothers were playing with on Saturday evening when Mrs. Murphy, out of the goodness of her heart, invited you three into her home. Now, maybe you kids saw the suit of armour as a play thing, but I assure you, it is a very valuable and historic artefact and is not a toy.

As for the painting, we know that one of the Shanahan brothers thought it funny and probably wanted it as a poster for his bedroom wall, but it is actually worth thousands of euros and should not be treated as a poster.

There was also over a thousand euros in cash taken. So here's the deal. You confess now, tell us where the painting, the armour suit and the cash is, and I'll recommend to the judge that you don't go to a juvenile detention centre."

"But we didn't steal anything!" declared Cathal forcibly, his voice trembling and tears welling up in his eyes. "Granda, you have to believe me!"

"Cathal," said Detective O'Grady sternly. "You had been in the house on Saturday evening, approximately twenty four hours before the crime took place. You clearly showed an interest in some of the items stolen. You were seen entering the grounds of the estate yesterday, shortly before the burglary occurred. You have become familiar with how to access the estate and the house. You can't get a single soul to vouch for you that they saw you any time after you were seen going into the estate yesterday. And now you expect me to believe that you're innocent, especially with your record of activity with the Shanahan brothers? You must think I came down in the last shower!

My advice to you Cathal would be to go home, sit down, have a good think about things and decide what you're going to do next."

"So you're letting me go?"

"Yes. You're free to go for now."

"But why would you do that if the Shanahans had supposedly confessed or hung me out to dry?"

"That's none of your business!"

"It is my business, 'cause I bet you they said nothing, 'cause they couldn't have!"

"That's enough guff out of you!" interjected Granda, rising to his feet. "Come on, the man said to go, now listen to what you're told for a change."

Granda caught Cathal by the back of his collar and brought him to his feet, before leading him out of the interview room and out the station door to where Garda Jim was waiting in the patrol car on the side of the street. As Cathal was leaving, he looked around for the Shanahans but they were nowhere to be seen. The car was silent the whole way from Killcrown Station to Granda's cottage, with the only words coming as Granda thanked the Garda for the drive when they arrived in the back yard, before the Garda went on his way again. It was now late afternoon and once they got in the door of the cottage, Granda filled a glass with cold water from the kitchen tap and put two slices of plain brown bread on a side plate. Turning to Cathal, he handed the bread and water to him and ordered him to go to his bedroom, with a specific instruction not to re-emerge until the next morning.

Cathal did as he was told, not having the energy to protest his innocence any further. That night, he would go over the events and allegations of the day a thousand times in his head and would sleep very little. He was desperate for morning to arrive, so he could get to school to meet the Shanahan brothers to discuss their dilemma and plan a solution.

CHAPTER 8
THE PLAN

The Shanahan brothers arrived in the classroom just in time for the start of proceedings, having been driven to school by their mother. This meant that they did not have an opportunity to discuss their predicament with Cathal since the Gardaí arrived at the school the previous day.

"HISTORY was made here at St. Joseph's National School yesterday," declared The Master, who stood in front of the blackboard as the children took their seats following Morning Prayer.

"Yes, history was made, but, alas, it was history for all the wrong reasons. You see, amongst our tightly knit school family, we have a criminal element. For the first time ever, the law enforcement agency of the State, An Garda Síochána, The Police, had to enter our educational paradise here at St. Joseph's, bringing shame and negativity on our school."

Throughout this lecture, Cathal, Billy and Barty sat at their respective seats, feeling all the eyes in the classroom on them for the second day in a row. They were disgusted with the antics of The Master, who was clearly trying to alienate them amongst their peers, and was being totally prejudicial in relation to the crimes they were suspected of having committed.

"So much for innocent until proven guilty," thought Cathal.

The Master continued:

"I've been teaching for a long time. As an experienced educationalist, I have seen many faces before me in this classroom. Some faces were bright, some were not so bright, some were nice people and some were not so nice. Most were average, forgettable really. But, none, and I repeat, NONE, were criminals!"

Some of the children, the "brainwashable" ones as Billy would describe them, shook their heads and tutted in sympathy with The Master.

"In all my years, I have never felt the disappointment and the hurt that I felt yesterday when Garda Jim O'Sullivan came to the door of this classroom. To make things worse, the sanctity of my own office, my oasis of calm and inspiration, has been contaminated after having served as a make shift interrogation room!"

"It's only ever been an interrogation room!" blurted Billy, who finally snapped. He had been prepared to put up with The Master's prejudice, and even his labelling of the boys as criminals, but The Master's reference to his office as an oasis of inspiration was just too much to tolerate, especially given that Billy had so many bad memories of the place.

Cathal and Barty had been bracing themselves in anticipation of a reaction from Billy, but had carried faint hopes that he would keep his composure and remain silent. Now, they both dropped their heads in frustration, knowing that The Master would punish Billy disproportionately for his outburst.

"Aw, Billy, as I expected, your little brush with the law hasn't taught you anything. You can write me a 500 word essay today during lunchtime entitled *My Trip to the Garda Station*," said a smiling Master, as he stared at Billy, who was trying desperately not to respond further, knowing that another outburst would land him even more punishment. Try as he might though, Billy just could not resist temptation.

"The Garda Station was a more pleasant experience than any day I ever spent here anyway!"

"Umm, I was expecting that too. Write about that in the sequel to your story during lunchtime tomorrow. We'll call that *My Trip to the Garda Station 2*."

"I suppose you'll be looking for me to do *Part 3* on Thursday?"

"Yes, Billy. And while you're at it, I'd be interested in seeing *Part 4* on Friday!"

"Just keep your mouth shut Billy!" shouted a voice, an intervention from Billy's younger brother, Barty.

"Barty, you can join your brother," instructed The Master in a cold response.

"For what?" asked Barty, "I was only trying to help?"

"I certainly don't need help from the likes of you," replied The Master.

"So, I have to stay in and write a story today?"

"Yes, and tomorrow and Thurday and Friday."

"Ah for God's sake!" blurted Cathal, outraged at the injustice being dispensed by The Master.

"You can join them too Cathal," quipped The Master, as Billy bowed his head in defeat, with Barty now beginning to sob, and Cathal just shaking his head in disbelief.

"Now, everybody, take out your geography books!" instructed The Master, grinning from ear to ear.

The classroom of children obeyed the order without question. The insurgency from the three rebels had been crushed mercilessly. A dejected Cathal reached into his bag for his geography text book, but as he did, he caught a glance from the girl seated at the desk next to his. Daisy McCarthy, the prettiest girl in the school, looked at him with a sympathetic smile and a little wink, as if to say that she knew he was being wronged. Cathal smiled back instinctively. For a brief moment, the first moment in a whole twenty four hours, Cathal felt good about himself. His world was crumbling around him but a nice smile and a wink from Daisy was enough to remind him that life isn't made up of just all bad things.

Daisy was the daughter of the local publican, Mossy McCarthy. She was much taller than all the other girls in her class and all the boys thought that she was gorgeous, with her long blonde hair and a tan that one would not normally find in County Kerry in December. Of course, some of the girls did not like the fact that all of the boys were crazy about Daisy, so some of them could be quite nasty to her at times. Cathal was happy to be sitting next to her.

The Master's geography lesson was heavily laden with waffle, as he embarked on tangent after tangent, discussing everything from the height of Mount Everest to the volume of water in the Nile Delta. Cathal pondered why they even needed text books, as The Master never made use of them anyway. Throughout the class, most of Cathal's attention was elsewhere, consumed by issues such as the trouble he was in with the Gardaí and the prospect of a full week of lunchtime detention. As the class progressed, a new distraction entered the fray. That distraction was Daisy.

As The Master was trying, but failing miserably, to accurately describe the sound made by a didgeridoo, Cathal noticed that Daisy was writing something on a piece of paper. Then he saw her fold the paper and a few seconds later, the paper arrived on his desk. Taking great care not to be seen by The Master, Cathal read the note:

I overheard Dad talking to customers in the bar last night. He said it wasn't ye!

Daisy watched as Cathal read the note and she smiled when he smiled at the content. He thought about writing a note of reply and that it would be discourteous not to, but then figured that knowing his luck, he would probably get caught and would get Daisy into trouble too, and he certainly did not want that to happen. Instead, he just smiled at her again, at which point she shyly looked away and pretended to be interested in The Master's ludicrous enactment of the movements of a kangaroo.

When lunchtime arrived, The Master and the children rushed out to the school yard, leaving the troublesome trio behind to begin recording on paper their tales of incarceration and interrogation. As soon as they were alone, they began discussing their predicament.

"Jaysus lads, we're in deep trouble," Billy declared. "This is serious."

"Serious!" exclaimed Cathal, "I'd say very serious."

"Very, very serious," added Barty for good measure.

"Seriously lads," continued Billy, "we're going to have to come up with a good plan to get out of this one."

"Any suggestions?" invited Cathal.

"Well, I was thinking that we could offer to take lie detector tests," suggested Barty.

"You'd probably fail yours," Billy snapped back wittily.

"Well you tell me something better Billy if you're so smart?" demanded Barty.

"Okay, I will so," answered Billy, as his younger brother and Cathal sat up in their seats. Billy began.

"I was doing a lot of thinking last night. You know our former business contact in town, the builder?"

"You mean the dodgy builder Billy," interrupted Cathal.

"Ya. Willie O'Brien. It's because he is dodgy that I think he can help us."

"I don't like where this is going Billy," sighed Barty.

"Just hear me out. You see, dodgy guys like Willie usually know lots of other dodgy guys and maybe, just maybe, he might be able to help us track down the items that were stolen from Mrs. Murphy."

"That's your plan?" said Cathal dismissively after a brief silence.

"That's the worst plan ever," added Barty. "If I came up with that Billy, you'd say I'm thick."

"You are thick. The point is, this guy probably moves in the same circles as the petty criminals that stole the stuff from Mrs. Murphy."

"Hang on a minute Billy," interrupted Cathal. "You're expecting this guy, who owes us nothing and if anything, has very good reason to dislike us a lot, you're expecting him to be our private detective?"

"When you put it that way Cathal, yes."

"A private detective?" blurted Barty. "That's just so stupid. You have to pay private detectives and what are we going to pay him with?"

"It's not what we're actually going to pay him with, it's what we'll promise we'll pay him with. Anyway, he won't actually know that he's doing the job of a private detective, he'll think he's just helping us out and helping himself in the process."

Cathal and Barty were confused but with some more detailed explanation of the plan by Billy, and with no alternative plan forthcoming, all three boys agreed that it was their only option. They decided to go with it, believing that even if it failed, things couldn't get any worse.

CHAPTER 9
PLACING THE ORDER

Willie O'Brien was one of those people who just couldn't stay out of trouble. No matter where he went or what he did, trouble seemed to follow him everywhere and would inevitably catch up with him every time. After his most recent scrape with the law, Willie swore to himself that he was going straight. He promised himself that he would never again delve into the murky world of illegality. He made a solemn vow to himself that for the rest of his days, he would be a model citizen, would pay his own way, would contribute to community and would be an all-round better person.

It was Tuesday afternoon, and Willie was driving through town in his work van. From time to time, Willie would get small construction jobs to do, like fixing a leaking roof or laying a footpath or painting a wall. He was also a man that would buy and sell various items and try to make a small profit on the transactions. It didn't really matter what items, once a profit could be made, he would be interested. On this particular Tuesday, Willie was on the way to repair some windows when his mobile phone rang. Not recognising the number, Willie answered the call, hoping that it would be a new customer with some job request that would provide some remuneration.

"Hallo," shouted Willie, his voice competing with the loud hum from his well-travelled engine.

"Is this Willie O'Brien?" asked the young male caller.

"Who's asking?"

"This is Billy Shanahan."

"Billy Shanahan! Billy Shanahan from Ballycastle?"

"Ya. How're you Willie?"

"What could you possibly want from me boyeen? Is this some sort of a trap or something? Am I being recorded or something?"

"Calm down Willie! It's no trap. I just need your help!"

"You need my help? With what? Nothing illegal I hope? I'm gone 100% clean now you know!"

"I assure you that it's nothing illegal."

"Well what is it then?"

"Well, Willie. You see, our local church roof is leaking and we're holding a fundraising Christmas concert to get money to fix it this weekend. Anyway, we're looking for some props for one of the comedy sketches on the night and we can't get what we're looking for anywhere, so we thought that you might be a good man to ask, since you have a lot of good contacts in the trading world."

"Well I do have a lot of contacts, you're right about that, but what's in it for me?"

"Well if you can get the things we're looking for, we'll pay for them and as soon as the concert is over, we'll give them to you, free of charge to do what you like with them. How does that sound to you?"

"It sounds too good to be true. Where's the catch?"

"There's no catch Willie. And better still, if we raise the

money to fix the roof, you might even be contracted to do the job?"

"Alright so, what are ye looking for?"

"Well, we're planning to put on a little sketch about King Arthur and the Knights of the Round Table, so we're looking for a knight's suit of armour and a shield and a sword. Do you think you could get those things for us?"

"A suit of armour wouldn't be too easy to get?"

"That's why we're calling you Willie. Could you try your best for us?"

"I'll try sure. I'll make a few calls. If I get ye sorted, will I definitely get to fix that roof?"

"I can't say for absolute definite at this stage Willie. All I will say is that, Fr. O'Rourke and I are very close. I'm the main choir singer in the parish and if I put in a good word, it'll carry a lot of weight."

"Okay then. Leave it with me. Give me a ring again tomorrow."

"Okay, thanks Willie. Bye bye."

Willie pressed the end call button and was just about to put the phone back on the passenger seat of the van when he noticed the flashing blue lights of the Garda Traffic Corps in his wing mirrors. The vigilant Garda promptly pulled Willie over and issued him with a €60 fine and two penalty points for using a mobile phone whilst driving. Guys like Willie just can't get a break!

CHAPTER 10
A VILLAGE DIVIDED

When Billy hung up the handset of the payphone at the back of Ted Hanratty's little grocery shop, Cathal and Barty were very excited and congratulated him heartily on the "professional" way that he got Willie O'Brien on board with their plan. Cathal paid particular tribute to Billy's false reference to being the head of the choir. All three boys had been huddled around the earpiece and were glad that, finally, they seemed to be making some progress in their attempts to clear their names. The plan was a long shot, but the boys hoped that Willie would check with his extensive list of contacts for the suit of armour and the shield and sword. They believed that there surely wouldn't be any other similar items going around, and that whoever burgled Mrs. Murphy's home would more than likely want to get rid of the stolen items without delay. They thought that if Willie could track down the stolen gear, they would have a chance of clearing their names.

Returning to the main part of the shop, the boys stopped to talk with Ted, who was now in his seventies but was still the friendliest and most genuine shopkeeper in all of Ireland.

"How's everything going anyway Ted?" asked Billy.

"Ah, just grand lads. A bit better for me than for ye I'd say?"

"You can say that again Ted!" replied Barty with a sigh.

"Look I know it wasn't ye and a good few people around the place believe the same thing too."

"Thanks very much Ted," replied Cathal, with a smile of consolation. "It's important to us to hear that. It's just a pity that my own grandfather doesn't believe me."

"Or our mother either," added Barty.

"Well, that's where ye might be behind the times a small bit lads. They both came in here today at separate times and I had a good chat with both of them. I told them that ye are good kids and they always knew that, but I think their judgement was a small bit clouded by all the recent hype and they jumped to conclusions about ye. I think I might have changed their minds."

Ted had barely the words out of his mouth and the boys hadn't time to thank him when the shop door burst open and in bounded Peggy Moore.

"So Ted, I see you're serving hardened criminals nowadays!" declared Peggy at the top of her voice.

"Now Peggy, don't you start. These boys are innocent."

"If I was in charge of the country, I'd have the six hands cut off the three of them!"

"Well first of all, humans have only two hands, not six and second of all, you're not in charge of the country," responded Billy sharply.

"Thank God she's not in charge," added Barty.

"Oh ye're cheeky brats the two of ye Shanahans. And ye've ruined Mick Kavanagh's only grandson. An orphan thief ye've made of him. He's like Oliver Twist now!"

Cathal rolled his eyes to heaven, more amused than

offended by the outright insensitivity of this woman. Ted took a more hardened position though.

"Now, Peggy. I'm warning you. You can't come in here and talk to any of my customers like that or if you do, I'll have to refuse you service in future."

The boys smiled. Peggy took a step back and the tone of her voice lowered and the pace of her speech slowed.

"I'd be very careful if I were you Ted Hanratty. If you keep talking to me like that, you'll be losing a very good grocery customer."

"Ha. You've all the signs of it!" goaded Billy, referring to Peggy's large size.

"We'll see how smart the three of ye are when the judge sends ye all to prison on Spike Island!"

"Well if they tried sending you Peggy, the boat would sink on the way out," snapped Cathal with a smile, as Ted and the Shanahan brothers broke into loud laughter.

"Come on lads, let's get out of here," declared Billy, as the three boys made for the door and bid goodbye to Ted, with Peggy slamming the door after them as they left.

"Could they really send us to prison on Spike Island?" asked Barty innocently as they walked away from the shop.

"No Barty," answered Cathal. "They closed that place down years ago. Don't be listening to that aul' windbag Peggy Moore!"

"Well at least Ted believes us," remarked Billy.

"Yeah. And Mossy McCarthy believes us too," added Cathal.

"And how do you know that?" quizzed Barty.

"Daisy told me."

"Oh, Daisy told you did she?" teased Billy. "When were you talking to the lovely Daisy?"

"Well I wasn't talking to her exactly. She wrote it in a note to me."

"A note!" exclaimed the brothers simultaneously, before teasing Cathal the whole way home about his emerging friendship with Daisy. While they were both a little envious, they enjoyed seeing Cathal get embarrassed about the subject. Amidst all their troubles and the challenges that lay ahead, the boys still managed to laugh and joke.

Deep down, all of them were hoping desperately for a breakthrough and for their innocence to be proven.

That night, at home, Cathal sat down with Granda for a long conversation. Perhaps somewhat influenced by the words of Ted Hanratty, Granda questioned Cathal about the burglary at the Murphy Estate and finally concluded that he was prepared to give the boys the benefit of the doubt.

"Cathal, I may have jumped to conclusions at the start and I'm sorry for that. I'm putting my trust in you and I hope you're not lying to me," declared Granda.

"You can trust me Granda. We're 100% innocent and we're going to prove it."

A similar conversation and outcome occurred in the Shanahan household. The tide was starting to turn in favour of the boys but they still needed proof of their innocence and that would be difficult to find.

Ted Hanratty's Shop

CHAPTER 11
A LEAD

Wednesday was an uneventful day in St. Joseph's National School. Most of the day was spent rehearsing for the upcoming Christmas concert, which was now only three days away. Boring and all as the rehearsals were, the day seemed to pass quicker than a regular day of tuition from the insufferable Master Seán Ó Luing.

As soon as the school day finished at 3pm, Cathal, Billy and Barty rushed to Ted Hanratty's shop to phone Willie O'Brien to find out if he had made any progress on tracking down the suit of armour or the other "props" that the boys had requested. After a quick whip around, Billy raised the 50 cent needed to pay for the call. 20 cent came from Cathal and 30 cent was his own contribution. Barty told them that he had no money. Billy dialled Willie's number.

"Hallo."

"Hi Willie. This is Billy Shanahan."

"Billy. I was hoping you'd call. I have good news for you boy."

"Good news?" exclaimed Billy with excitement in his voice, as Cathal and Barty's eyes lit up.

"Ya. I know where you can get your stuff."

"That's mighty Willie. Where?"

"There's a fella in Limerick who has exactly what you're looking for. Give him a ring and you can arrange to meet up with him."

"What's his name Willie?"

"I don't know that. I was just given his number by a fella I know, who knows another fella I know."

Willie called out a mobile phone number to Billy, while Cathal, who was listening to the call, promptly and excitedly jotted it down on the inside cover of a copybook after pulling a pencil from his school bag. Billy thanked Willie sincerely and before ending the call, promised him again that he would get the items after the concert to do what he pleased with them. Willie also reminded Billy that he wanted to get the job of fixing the church roof, and Billy reassured him that he would "do his best on that one".

All along, Cathal and Barty had been highly sceptical of Billy's idea of involving Willie O'Brien, but now they were beginning to believe that the plan might actually work and were visibly excited.

"I told ye Willie could help," boasted Billy before asking Cathal for more money for the payphone.

"I've nothing else left, sorry Billy," responded Cathal, turning his trouser pockets inside out as proof.

"Barty, are you sure you haven't got any money?" Billy asked his younger brother, who had a guilty look on his face.

"This was my sweets money," protested Barty, as he produced a 50 cent piece from his pocket, to the annoyance of Cathal and Billy.

Slotting the 50 cent piece in the payphone, Billy nervously dialled the number that he had just been given. A man answered with a brash and blunt tone.

"Yeah?"

"Hello."

"Who's this?"

"Hello. My name is Billy Shanahan. I'm calling from Ballycastle in County Kerry about a suit of armour and a shield and sword."

"Oh right yeah."

"Am, how much are you selling them for?"

"You want the lot?"

"Yes please."

"A thousand."

Billy was taken aback. Although he knew the stolen items were deemed to be valuable, he hadn't really thought about the sums involved.

"A thousand you say?"

"That's what I said."

"Okay, right. Can you do any better than that?"

"Do you want them or not?"

"I do yeah."

"Well that's the price. Take them or leave them."

Billy's gut was telling him that he was wading into waters far beyond his depth, but given the trouble that he and the boys found themselves in, he felt that he had no alternative but to completely follow through on his plan. In his mind, he knew a place where he could access cash like that at short notice.

"Okay, I'll take them."

"When can you pick them up?"

"Well, actually, I was hoping you could deliver them if that would be possible?"

"It'll cost you another €100."

"Another €100. Well alright then. When can you deliver them?"

"When do you need them?"

"As soon as possible. Can you do it tonight?"

"I can do it tonight but it'll cost you another €100 at this short notice."

"So that's €1,200 total," confirmed Billy, as Cathal and Barty stood by his side looking very worried by the direction the conversation was taking.

"Ya. Where do you want me to drop them to?"

"Okay. Do you know Ballycastle."

"Yeah."

"Right. Do you know the Community Hall?"

"Ya."

"Well our fundraising Christmas concert is on there on Saturday night and these are props for the concert, so can you meet us in the carpark there?"

"Whatever kid. What time?"

"Is 9pm okay?"

"See you there."

The man hung up.

"We're on tonight lads," declared Billy, with a mixture of excitement, worry and nervousness in his voice and in his demeanour.

"Hang on a minute Billy," protested Cathal. "This is all spiralling out of control a bit. First of all, where on earth are we going to get €1,200 by 9pm tonight? Secondly, this guy could be some lunatic for all we know and you want us to meet him in the darkness of night in an isolated carpark? Thirdly, this might not even be the stuff that was stolen from Mrs. Murphy and where will we be left then, and lastly, shouldn't we go to the Gardaí now?"

"Yeah," added Barty.

"Yeah what?" asked Billy, confronting his brother.

"Yeah, I agree with Cathal."

"Listen. It's quite simple. I can get the €1,200. That's not a problem."

"From where?" pried Cathal.

"I have a rainy day fund at home. We can use that."

"Right, even though I find that hard to believe, what if this guy's a nut job and bundles you or me or Barty for that matter into his van in the dark of night?"

"That's where my plan comes in. Firstly, the carpark is well lit with street lights and second of all, only two of us will be there for the transaction."

"Where will the third person be?" inquired Barty.

"The third person will be hidden, recording the whole thing with a video camera. The area will be well enough lit to pick up what's happening, the video will be the proof that we need to clear our names, and if anything goes wrong, the third person can run away and call for help."

"But what if it's not the stuff that was stolen from Mrs. Murphy?" pressed Cathal. "Or would you even know the difference?"

"The shield in Mrs. Murphy's house had a distinctive red cross on it. If it's the wrong stuff, we'll know straight away. Anyway, what are the chances of there being another suit of armour knocking around in the petty criminal world?"

"But if it is the wrong stuff?" asked Barty.

"Well, if it's the wrong stuff, we pay the guy €200 for his trouble, leave the stuff with him and send him back on his way and take the loss on the chin. It's a small gamble for our reputations and good names."

"But why don't we just go to the Gardaí now, since we know that this guy will be coming here tonight with what is probably the stolen gear?" insisted Cathal.

"We can't go to the guards," snapped Billy. "A, they won't believe us, B, knowing them, they'll scare him off before he arrives and C, I want to prove that three boys of our age did a better job investigating this case and solving it than them, and show them and everybody else up for being so quick to point the finger of blame at us."

By that point in the debate, Billy was talking and thinking at the same time, but he had done just about enough to convince Cathal and Barty that his plan was worth pursuing.

"I'm not 100% sure about this Billy, but I'm willing to trust you on this one," said Cathal.

"Ya, I'm the same," added Barty. "There's something telling me that this could all go horribly wrong, but I don't think we have much of a choice anymore."

"Okay then. It's settled," confirmed Billy. "Trust me guys, by tonight, our names will be cleared and everyone around here will be eating huge slices of humble pie. There's only one more thing we have to get."

"What's that?" asked Barty.

"A video camera," said Billy. "But I know where we can get one - The Master's office!"

Ballycastle remained one of the few place in the entire developed world that still did not have mobile phone coverage. Located in a valley surround by the Slieve Gaum Mountains, The McCarthy Reeks Mountains and the sea, Ballycastle's topography was not conducive to modern wireless communications networks, so none of the three boys used mobile phones. To record the handover of the stolen items, they would need to "borrow" the video camera from the school. It being a Wednesday, the boys were in luck, as the school stayed open late on Wednesdays to allow the cleaning lady, Mrs. Foley, to come in and carry out her weekly tasks.

Arriving back to the school, the boys could see that Mrs. Foley's car was parked outside the gate and that the front door was wide open. Following a brief discussion, it was decided that Barty would be the one to try to sneak in and snatch the video camera from The Master's office. Cathal and Billy hid inside the gate of the field across the road from the school, while Barty embarked on his mission. Having looked in all directions to see that nobody was watching as he went through the gate, Barty made a dash for the front door, stopping briefly when he got there to peep inside. From his vantage point, he could see that Mrs. Foley was working in Miss O'Shea's classroom.

"This is my chance," he thought, as he carefully crept his way along the corridor, sneaking past the room where Mrs. Foley was vacuuming, continuing as far as The Master's office. Pressing down on the door handle, he couldn't believe his luck when it opened. Until that moment, it hadn't occurred to Barty that he didn't have a plan if the door turned out to be locked. As he entered the office, he gave a quick glance all around to make sure that he wasn't being watched, before closing the door behind him. Barty was no stranger to The Master's office, having been summonsed there for questioning and punishment on a regular basis over the seven years that he had so far spent in St. Joseph's. Knowing the layout of the office so well helped him to find the video camera without any great difficulty. It had been sitting in its case on a shelf behind The Master's desk and Barty removed the camera from the case and placed it in his school bag, putting the empty case back on the shelf. A small window looked out from the office onto the front yard of the school towards the school gate. From there, Barty could see Cathal and Billy, who by now were on the look out to make sure that the coast was clear for Barty to emerge from the school. He stood closer to the window and when Billy and Cathal caught sight of him, gave him the thumbs up sign and beckoned to him that the coast was clear. Barty signalled back and turned to leave the office, but as he did, a small cardboard box on a shelf in the corner caught his eye. It wasn't so much the box but the writing on the box that caught his attention:

5th Class Christmas Exams

Knowing that he was pushing his luck and that he had to get out of there as quickly as possible, Barty decided not to look in the box and had his hand on the door handle, about to leave, when he stopped and looked back at the box. Like a magnet pulling metal, Barty was drawn back to it, and he couldn't stop himself from looking inside. There in the box lay numerous copies of a paper which along the top read:

St. Joseph's N.S.
Christmas Exam
5th Class

Barty was torn between whether to leave the exam paper after him or whether to sneak a quick peep at it. In the end, not having enough time to read it all, he carefully took one of the papers and stuffed it into his school bag, before quickly leaving the office, gently pulling the door closed behind him. He looked along the corridor to see where Mrs. Foley was but couldn't see her anywhere. The sound of the vacuum cleaner could nolonger be heard, and Barty was unsure whether to turn back into the office or make a dash for the exit. He decided to do the later but just as he reached the front door, Mrs. Foley walked in through it and the pair collided, knocking each other backwards to the ground.

"Barty Shanahan, you eejit!" exclaimed Mrs. Foley, as she got back on her feet. "What are you doing here at this hour of the evening and sure you know you shouldn't be running in the corridor."

"I'm sorry Mrs. Foley. I forgot my, ah, my…French book."

"French book? But ye don't study French in primary school?"

"Am, no, did I say French? I meant Maths. I always mix up the two."

"Hmm, I hope you're not up to any mischief. You're in enough trouble as it is from what I hear."

"No. I was just leaving."

"Go on, get out of here."

"Bye Mrs. Foley."

Barty ran to the school gate, where he was met by Cathal and Billy. He would have preferred to have not been seen by Mrs. Foley but the main thing for Barty was that he managed to get the video camera.

"Did you get the camera?" asked Billy.

"I sure did boys."

Cathal and Billy warmly congratulated Barty before the three boys made their way home. Cathal took possession of the video camera, being the most technologically savvy of the three. They all agreed to meet at their usual meeting place, at the bottom of the bohereen leading to Granda's house, at exactly 8.45pm, from where they would proceed to the Community Hall to set up the surveillance camera in advance of the handover.

CHAPTER 12
ACTION

Cathal hadn't slept very well on Monday or Tuesday night, mainly due to mental anguish caused by the trouble that he found himself in. By the time he arrived home from school on Wednesday, he felt extremely tired, and not even the impending excitement of the handover of the stolen goods could prevent him from wanting to take a short nap. At 6pm, when Cathal and Granda had finished dinner, Cathal went to his room to lie down. He planned to rest for about a half an hour, after which he planned to learn how to use the video camera, before getting ready to meet the Shanahans. As he turned off the light and lay back on his bed, his school uniform still on, Cathal felt his entire body relax and sink into the mattress. He was asleep in a matter of seconds.

Unfortunately for Cathal, what was intended to be a nap lasting no more than a half an hour, turned into a three hour sleep. When Cathal woke, a little confused in the complete darkness, he had to think for a few moments before realising what day it was. Then turning to his bedside clock radio, to his horror he saw that it was 8.55pm. He was to have met the Shanahans ten minutes earlier and should have left Granda's cottage a further few minutes before that. He was extremely late, and now the whole plan was jeopardised. He rushed to his feet and quickly put on his shoes, taking great care not to make too much noise and alert Granda in the process. Grabbing his school bag, with the video camera inside, he tiptoed down the stairs and ever so quietly unlocked the front door and ran out into the night.

Cathal ran all the way through the darkness to the Community Hall. As he left Granda's bohereen, he was lucky not to be struck by a passing car, which had to swerve to avoid him as Cathal showed scant regard for his own safety in his haste. He was totally breathless when he got to the carpark where Billy and Barty were still waiting. Worse than the breathlessness was the realisation, when he reached there, that the man with the stolen gear had come and gone. The Shanahans had handed over the money in return for the armour suit, shield and sword, but the whole transaction had not been recorded, which was the primary objective of the entire operation.

"Where the hell were you?" shouted Billy to Cathal angrily, with the stolen items on the ground beside him.

"I'm so sorry lads, I fell asleep and only just woke up," spluttered Cathal, trying to catch his breath as he came to a halt beside his friends.

"You're after ruining this whole plan Cathal," complained Barty, who was calmer than Billy but still very disappointed and angry with Cathal.

"I know, I know. I'm sorry guys. I didn't mean it. I just slept!"

"Just slept? Just slept? You more than just slept. You're after costing us a small fortune, and now we're in possession of stolen goods with no proof of how we got them," shouted

Billy. "I took the money from my mother's safe at home and when she finds out it's gone, she'll go ballistic!"

"I thought you said you had a rainy day fund!" observed Cathal.

"Well I bloody lied because I thought I'd only be borrowing the money for a few hours!" Billy shouted again.

For a moment, Cathal was afraid of Billy, such was the look of anger on his face, but that fear became much worse when the boys saw the lights of a car approaching the Community Hall. As it drew closer to them, to their absolute shock, a siren sounded with flashing blue lights appearing on the roof of the car. It was Garda Jim O'Sullivan and the boys were now in far more serious trouble than before. All the pleading and explaining in the world wouldn't prevent the Garda from arresting all three of the boys for possession of stolen goods. As they were being placed in the rear seat of the Garda patrol car, Peggy Moore arrived on the scene and got out of her car.

"Thanks for the tip off Peggy," said Garda Jim. "We'd never have caught them without you."

"I knew they were up to no good when I saw young Kavanagh on the move Jim," replied Peggy. "He was lucky I didn't drive over him. Ran straight out in front of me so he did."

It was then that Cathal realised that it was Peggy Moore that had almost hit him with her car, and that not only had he messed up the entire operation, but he had also drawn the attention of the Gardaí on it. For the second time in just over forty eight hours, the three boys found themselves in Killcrown Garda Station. This time though, all three were charged with burglary, breaking and entering and possession of stolen goods, including an armour suit, a shield a sword and a video camera.

Ballycastle Community Hall

CHAPTER 13
MORE BAD NEWS

Cathal hadn't slept all night and turned on the radio beside his bed just in time for the morning news.

Good morning, you're listening to Kingdom FM, it's 8 o'clock on Thursday December 19th, 2013, here is the news:

Gardaí in Killcrown last night arrested and charged three youths in connection with a burglary at a residence in the locality last weekend.

It is understood that most of the items that were taken from the house were recovered during the arrest. Gardaí also recovered equipment that had earlier been taken from a local primary school. The three youths will appear at a special court sitting at a later date and their identities cannot be reported for legal reasons. However, all three are believed to be from the Ballycastle area.

The following audio clip is of local woman, Peggy Moore, who spoke to Kingdom FM and told us how the dramatic events unfolded last night:

I was driving to Bingo when I noticed unusual movements from a youth dressed in dark clothing. Without even thinking of my own personal safety, I immediately alerted our local Garda, who was on the scene within minutes and hunted down these three dangerous thieves and their stolen loot, with my assistance of course.

Everyone in Ballycastle is breathing a sigh of relief, now that these criminals have been apprehended, thanks in no small part to myself.

It's like the whole place has been under siege from a spree of crime in recent times and now hopefully things will return to normality.

Did I mention that they wouldn't have been caught only for me?

~

There will be news in full on Kingdom FM at 9 o'clock and the time now is two minutes past eight.

Cathal turned off the radio again.

"Nobody better than Peggy Moore to twist a story!" he thought.

CHAPTER 14
THE GREAT ESCAPE

News travels fast in Ballycastle, and bad news travels even faster. By the time Cathal and the Shanahan brothers arrived at school on Thursday morning, the entire locality knew what had happened the previous night, and everyone was talking about it. Disapproving looks from parents dropping off their children met the boys at the school gate, and nearly all the children in the school completely shunned the trio.

One of the first reactions from The Master was to announce a minor change to the Christmas Nativity Play. The Three Wise Men, played by Cathal, Billy and Barty, would now become The Three Unwise Convicts and instead of gold, frankincense and myrrh, they would carry a sword, shield and video camera. The Master was fully intent on humiliating the three boys, and now they were dreading the concert on Saturday night.

The Master then proceeded to spend the first two hours of the school day delivering a sharply pointed lecture to the entire school assembly about values and crime, throwing in some bespoke lines such as:

"The commandment says: Thou shalt not steal. I say, thou shalt not speak to those who steal…"

"When we look around us at our school family, we see some people we would rather not have in our midst. Let us pray that they will go away soon…"

"Even during the famine, when people were starving to death in this locality, they did not steal video cameras from the school…"

The entire saga was now beginning to take a heavy emotional toll on all three of the boys, and during lunchtime detention, Barty became very upset. As Cathal and Billy were busy writing their 500 word punishment essay, *My Trip to the Garda Station 3*, Barty sat at the front of the room, staring out the window at the blue December sky.

"Hi Barty, start writing or Aul' Hairy Face will have you in here in January too!" warned Billy from the back of the classroom.

"Barty, get working," instructed Cathal from the middle row of desks.

"Barty, are you listening?" asked Billy.

But there was no response from Barty. Instead, he continued to stare into space, seemingly oblivious to his surroundings. Cathal and Billy looked at each other, concerned that the pressure had all become too much for Barty to handle and that he was about to break under the strain. They were right. Barty finally spoke, still staring in the same direction.

"Everywhere I go and everything I do for the rest of my life, they'll call me a thief."

Billy and Cathal considered interrupting him right there, but there was something about the solemn tone of his speech that made them hold their silence.

Barty continued:

"Everyone who meets me and even people who'll only know of me will call me a thief…If Dad was here, he'd fix it."

His shoulders then began to twitch and soon the twitching became heavy movements, and before Cathal and Billy knew it, Barty was wailing bitterly at his desk. The two boys rushed to his side to comfort him and try to calm him, but he was inconsolable. He struggled to draw his breath, such was his loss of self-control, and all Cathal and Billy could do was put their hands on his back and pat his shoulders.

Ten minutes passed and Barty was still balling his eyes out, loudly wailing, his face wet with tears. Cathal and Billy didn't know what to do. Lunch break would be over in a few minutes and everyone would be coming back into the classroom, and they didn't want Barty to be seen in such a vulnerable state.

"Right. Sod this. I'm getting him out of here," declared Billy.

"What do you mean?" asked Cathal.

"I'm getting him out of here, full-stop. This is no place for him in the state he's in, and I'll be dammed if I'm going to give Aul' Hairy Face the satisfaction of seeing him like this."

"So, you're just going to get up and go?"

"Yeah. Are you coming with us?"

Cathal thought for a moment about all the ramifications of breaking out of school, and about all of the trouble that he was already in, but then something inside him told him to just go with it, and that being at school was the wrong place for all of them at this time.

"Okay. I'm outa here too!" declared Cathal with a cheeky grin.

Billy smiled and turned his attention back to Barty, whose wails had by now become sobs.

"Barty, did you hear that. Young Kavanagh's finally after becoming a man and is going to escape from here with us? Come on Barty, we're getting out of here."

Barty turned to look at the boys, his eyes all red and bloodshot, his nose snotty, his cheeks wet and his voice trembling.

"But we can't just get out of here?"

"But we can, Barty, and we will," responded Billy, rising to his feet and lifting Barty to his feet too.

"But The Master will kill us," replied Barty.

"No he won't. He can't do that and he can't make things any worse for us. And I'm not going to stay here and be abused anymore, and I'm not going to leave my brother stay here for that either."

"That's the spirit Billy," cheered Cathal. "Do you hear that Barty, we're getting out of here?"

Barty smiled, as Billy and Cathal gathered their school bags and coats, and soon had his own coat on and his bag packed.

"So, are we going to sneak around to the back and over the fence at the back of the pump shed?" inquired Cathal of Billy.

"No, we're going straight out the door and straight past Aul Hairy Face and straight out the gate, and if he dares stop us, he'll regret it!"

Billy meant what he said and the three boys marched in a straight line out the door of the classroom, down the corridor, out the front door and into the yard. There The

Master confronted them but they just kept walking past him. He walked along beside Billy as far as the gate, at which point he stood in front of him, blocking his exit.

"You're not leaving these school grounds. When you're in here, you are under my control," declared The Master, with everyone in the school, including the other teacher, Miss O'Shea, now gathered around, watching the flashpoint unfold.

"Get out of our way," said Billy calmly, staring The Master straight in the eyes.

"I won't get out of your way. You turn back now and get back to the classroom," insisted The Master.

"Get out of our way now!" shouted Billy, a furious look coming to his face.

"You get back in the classroom right now, you little thief!" shouted The Master in reply, before aggressively grabbing Billy by his ear and holding it tightly.

It would be the last time that Master Seán Ó Luing would lay a hand on Billy Shanahan. As soon as he made contact with his ear, before Miss O'Shea even had time to intervene, Billy clasped his fist and swung with all his might toward The Master, connecting directly in his gut, knocking him to the ground, gasping for air. Everyone looked on in amazement, but without saying another word, Billy, Cathal and Barty just marched out the school gate. As they walked away, Cathal could have sworn that he saw Miss O'Shea smile discreetly when he glanced over his shoulder to watch as The Master slowly got to his feet before walking back towards the school building in defeat.

There was no triumphalism on the walk home as may have been expected following such a dramatic episode. Things had become far too serious for that to happen. Instead the boys walked home in near silence, with Cathal accompanying the Shanahans to their home. From there, Billy made a phone call to his mother, who was at work, to explain to her what had happened and that he and Barty were safe. Cathal made a similar phone call to Granda, who was angry and instructed him to get home without delay. Barty told the boys that he was going to rest for a while and thanked them for looking after him, still somewhat embarrassed by his outpouring of emotion. Billy told Cathal he would walk with him back to Granda's and the pair chatted on the way.

"That was amazing what you did for your brother back at the school," remarked Cathal. "He's lucky to have you to look out for him."

"Barty is really very vulnerable underneath it all," replied Billy. It's been very hard for him since Dad died."

"Yeah. I know what you mean."

"Of course you do Cathal. I'm sorry. Sometimes I forget that I'm not the only one in the world to have lost a parent, not to mention my whole family."

"If you don't mind me asking, what happened your Dad Billy?"

"He died on a building site in England. He was on a section of scaffolding a few hundred feet up when the whole thing just collapsed and down he went with it. A good friend of his from Galway was on the same scaffold and died beside my father."

"That's just terrible. We can change the subject if you like."

"No, it's fine. I haven't really spoken about it until now to be honest, but I must have thought it over in my head a million times. In a way, it's liberating to talk about it."

"When my parents and Gearóid, that was my brother's name, when they died I just thought that my whole world had ended, and it has in one way, but life goes on and a different world goes on. It's amazing how talking helps. I've been going to a counsellor every so often since it happened. I think it helps."

"They wanted us to do that too but I said no way and when I said no, Barty said no. In a way, I kinda' feel guilty now that my refusal stopped Barty from taking up the offer. I just couldn't picture myself on one of those leather couches spilling my guts!"

"But sure it's not like that at all. It's very casual really. You should reconsider, even if just for Barty's sake. There are more ways of looking out for him than just clobbering his teacher you know!"

The boys laughed.

"Ya, I know," said Billy. "You know, Christmas is going to be a nightmare though. The last time we saw Dad was when he was leaving at the start of January. He was due to come home for a weekend at the start of February but he never made it. My mother finds it so hard to deal with everything and try to keep a brave face on for the younger kids, and now she has all our trouble to deal with too. I just wish we could find some way of getting the real truth to prove we're innocent."

"I know. I just always believe that the truth comes out in the end. No matter what, it does and everything happens for a reason. I think we just have to keep believing that. We're bound to get a lucky break and we just need to take it when it comes."

"Do you think a lot about your brother and parents?"

"All the time. Every waking hour. And even when I'm asleep, they're in my dreams. Sometimes I see my mother, sometimes she's with Dad, sometimes she's alone and sometimes it's just Gearóid. Then, I have dreams about when we were all together too. The weirdest thing ever is that every night since I heard the story, I've been dreaming about my great-great- granduncle, Micheál MacDiarmada and his Lady Evelyn. I see him lying in Murphy's Woods, all alone in the darkness. I can even see his face as clear as anything, and then I see her there in her room, looking out the window, playing her music. It's creepy. It's as if I can even hear her music!"

"Wow, that is weird. I know what you mean about the music though. Dad was a great guitar player, and I often hear his tunes in my head. I can't explain it. Do you really believe that stuff about Sean MacDiarmada's ghost in the cellar and Lady Evelyn and her music? Do you think we really heard her ghost?"

"At this stage, I'd believe anything."

The boys had reached the bottom of the bohereen leading to Granda's cottage, and Billy promptly stopped. He didn't want to go any further because he was afraid of the type of reception he might get from Cathal's grandfather. The boys bid each other farewell and agreed to meet at that same point on the way to school the following morning.

When Cathal came home from the Garda Station the previous night, he and Granda had a blazing row. Granda told Cathal that he was ashamed to call him his grandson and that Cathal had repeatedly betrayed his trust since he arrived to live with him. Granda said that Cathal had made him feel like a fool, after coming to believe his story about being innocent, only for Cathal and the Shanahans to be caught red handed a day later.

Cathal was naturally devastated to hear such words from his own grandfather, but an even more furious reception greeted him on this occasion. As far as Granda was concerned, under no circumstances at all should Cathal have left the school grounds before the end of the school day. Despite Cathal's explanation of the context of the decision to leave the school, Granda was having none of it.

"This arrangement just isn't working out Cathal. I'm too old to be dealing with this sort of thing. We're going to have to come up with some other plan for you, but I don't think you should stay here with me for much longer boy," he bellowed.

"But Granda, I'm innocent, and the Shanahans are innocent, and maybe if you helped me prove it instead of constantly jumping to conclusions, we wouldn't be having this argument!"

"Innocent? Help you? Jumping to conclusions? You must think that I'm am awful ape altogether boyeen! Well I'll tell you this much, you've pulled your last fast one on me! To think that two days ago you came home here and I sat you down after a lot of soul searching and told you that I believed you, and then, twenty four hours later, you told me you were going to bed when you were sneaking out of here to meet those other two thieves!"

"But they're not thieves and I'm not a thief!"

"Stop lying to me boy!"

"But I'm not lying Granda!"

"You are! Admit it!"

"I won't because it's the truth!"

"Well I'll tell you this much, there'll be no liar living under this roof. I'll start making calls in the morning about finding you someplace else to live and in the mean-time, stay away from those Shanahans. They're no good, and I won't have you or them bringing any more shame on my name!"

Granda stormed out of the house and drove away in his car in a fit of temper, faster than Cathal ever imagined he would see Granda drive a car. By 10pm, Granda still hadn't arrived home and Cathal went to bed.

Before getting into bed, Cathal knelt and prayed to his parents and brother for help. Never before had he found himself in such trouble. Not only had he lost his family and his home, but now he was in serious trouble with the law and was going to lose his new home. Things had never seemed so low for Cathal and he wondered if things would ever be right for him again. Between tears and prayers, he eventually fell asleep, wondering if it would be his last night in the little loft room in Granda's cottage.

CHAPTER 15
THE BEAUTIFUL LIGHT

Just after 2am, Granda somehow managed to direct the key into the lock to allow him to get in the back door of his cottage. Cathal had been woken by the sound of the engine of Mossy McCarthy's car, dropping Granda home from a late night in McCarthy's Bar. He listened as Granda stumbled his way in through the kitchen and living room and eventually into Granda's own bedroom, which was located in the front of the house at the bottom of the stairs. After a few moments of silence, Cathal decided to get out of bed and go downstairs to check that Granda was alright. He peeped in Granda's bedroom door just enough to see the old man lying fully clothed on his bed, already snoring heavily, despite having only been in bed a few minutes. Clearly Granda was after having a few too many at McCarthy's.

"That's his way of dealing with things," thought Cathal, closing the door of Granda's bedroom. After checking that the back door was locked, which it wasn't, and after turning off all the lights in the kitchen and living room, which Granda had left on, Cathal went back upstairs to his bedroom. Turning off the light, he went to the window for what he thought might be the last time he would stare out at the view that he had come to love in recent weeks. Nearly all the countryside was in darkness, with only the lights of Killcrown in the distance breaking the complete blackness. With no moon to light the scene, the River Clane and Ballycastle Harbour were invisible, and Cathal thought about the first time that he had looked out that window into the night, and about how so much had changed in the short few weeks since then.

At that very moment, as Cathal thought about Seánín Solas and the legend of his phantom light, he could not believe his eyes when a light appeared out of the darkness in the distance. The light was a beautiful bright orange colour with a circular glow surrounding it. It seemed to hover in the air over Murphy's Estate, just on the near side of the lights of the town of Killcrown. He watched in amazement, as the light just hung in the air in a stationary position. The instant he saw it, he knew it was a special light.

"This isn't happening!" thought Cathal. "I look out the window for thirty seconds and all of a sudden a mysterious light appears in the distance!"

He watched for at least an hour to see if the light would move or disappear or do anything else but it just stayed there. Strangely, Cathal wasn't afraid. In fact, he felt a warm feeling when he saw the light, the type of feeling that one gets when they see the first swallow of summer or witness a falling star. He thought about waking Granda to show him the light but then decided not to, given the problems they were having and the condition in which Granda arrived home. He even thought about running out and alerting the Shanahans to show them the light, but was afraid that he wouldn't get to wake them without waking their mother too, and that could have caused untold hassle for everyone. Eventually, he lay back into bed and thought about what the light could be and why it had appeared to him.

CHAPTER 16

THE WOODS AT NIGHT

It was just after 4am when Cathal arrived at Killcrown Slipway in his little boat. It was the first time ever that he had crossed the River Clane alone, and he was surprised at how well he managed to row across the waterway in the darkness. Up ahead, he could see the beautiful orange light still hovering over Murphy's Estate. After a few minutes, Cathal was running along the roadway outside the estate's perimeter wall, and was about to enter the woods at the usual point of access. Somewhere in the still of the night air, he could hear the sweet sound of the beautiful music of a flute. He glanced up at the light and seeing that it was just up ahead, he entered the woods. Soon he had reached the place where he and the Shanahans had been working, and the light was now just a very short distance away. As Cathal moved closer and closer, the light dropped lower and lower, until it eventually disappeared into the ground under one of the newly planted trees. Cathal was now standing alone in the woods in the depth of night, staring straight into the profoundly sorrowful looking face of a young man with piercing red eyes.

CHAPTER 17
THE BALLYCASTLE DERBY

Friday was full dress rehearsal day at school, meaning that Paddy, Granda's donkey, had to come to school with Cathal. Cathal left home on foot, walking beside Paddy, holding his reins as they went. Paddy was a friendly donkey and loved human company, but old age had now crept up on him. Cathal was being careful not to do anything that would in any way cause the animal distress or tire him out, and so walked very slowly all the way to school. When Cathal left home, Granda was still asleep, as Cathal had anticipated, given the state he was in when he arrived home in the small hours of the morning. All the way to school, Cathal wondered what type of day lay ahead following their walkout the previous day. For a while, he even contemplated not going to school, out of fear of being turned away at the door by The Master, but ultimately he decided to keep going and face his fears.

Cathal had almost reached the school when he heard a familiar voice call out his name from a distance behind him. It was Billy Shanahan, and he was running to catch up with Cathal, with Barty following Billy, but being unable to keep pace with him. Cathal stopped and waited for both of them.

"Morning donkeys!" hailed Billy with a smile.

"Hi guys," replied Cathal. "Not sure it's a good morning

though. We mightn't even be let in the gate after yesterday."

"You don't have to worry a thing about that Cathal my friend," replied Barty, breathlessly. "It's all under control."

"How's that?"

"Miss O'Shea called the Department of Education yesterday after we left and reported Aul Hairy Face for the incident in the yard," explained Billy. "Apparently the Department gave him his last warning, so something tells me he'll be on his best behaviour all day today."

Cathal was relieved, and hoped that Billy and Barty were right. It turned out that they were. When the boys arrived at the school gate, the first person to meet them there was The Master himself.

"Good morning boys," said The Master, with a forced smile that he struggled desperately to maintain.

The boys politely returned the greeting, as they walked past him into the school yard, with Paddy instantly attracting a crowd of the younger children, who gathered around him in awe, each of them wanting to pat the donkey's head or rub his soft coat. For a while, the three boys felt normal again, and it was as if everyone had forgotten about the crimes they were being associated with. Cathal tied Paddy up just outside the front door of the school and went inside with Billy and Barty. In the corridor, they met Miss O'Shea, who smiled at them as she passed. The boys smiled back, grateful for the kindness and responsibility she had shown in reporting The Master's aggressive behaviour.

Daisy McCarthy had been chosen to play the Virgin Mary in the Nativity play, so before the dress rehearsal could proceed, the first action of the day was to acquaint Paddy and Daisy. Once class had started, The Master instructed Cathal to accompany Daisy to the school yard to "get to know" Paddy.

Cathal was delighted with the chance to get out of the classroom and, more importantly, the chance to chat with Daisy. When they got outside, he untied Paddy and handed the reins to Daisy.

"Paddy, this is Daisy, Daisy, this is Paddy," said Cathal with a smile.

"Hello Paddy," said Daisy as she gently rubbed the side of Paddy's head before Paddy opened his wide mouth and gave Daisy a big affectionate lick of his long wet tongue, with Daisy initially squirming from the sensation before laughing loudly.

"That's so slimy," she exclaimed. "But he's so cute."

"Now Paddy, I want you to do everything Daisy wants," instructed Cathal, and as if he understood, Paddy replied with a loud neigh. Daisy laughed again and Cathal was delighted with the impression that Paddy was making.

"I'll have to bring Paddy everywhere I go," thought Cathal, such was his charm.

Daisy walked Paddy around the school yard for a few minutes, with Paddy following her when she moved and stopping when she stopped. As they walked, Daisy and Cathal chatted.

"Public opinion seems to have swung against ye after Wednesday night Cathal. I don't think my father still believes that ye're innocent anymore."

"I don't think anybody believes us at this stage Daisy. I'm even starting to doubt myself."

"I wouldn't say that so certainly".

"Well name one person who does believe us?"

"Daisy McCarthy."

Cathal was flabbergasted.

"You mean you believe us? You?"

"No. It's another Daisy McCarthy over the road. Yes, me. Why do you find that so hard to believe?"

"No reason. I'm just, ah, just surprised that anyone at all believes our story, especially after being caught with all the stuff."

"It looks really bad, I'll be straight with you. But, why don't the Gardaí just contact the man ye got the stuff off of and track him down that way?"

"We gave them the mobile phone number that we used to call him and the phone is dead. On top of that, Billy and Barty memorised the registration plates of the van, but it seems that no such plates were ever registered so they think we just made them up. The Gardaí even asked the guy who tracked him down in the first place but he isn't giving any information, probably because he's afraid of any retribution. So we're well and truly in trouble."

"Don't give up Cathal. The truth will come out. It always does."

"Thanks Daisy, that means a lot. That's what I always say too. By the way, why are you so certain of our innocence when everyone else thinks we're guilty?"

"I just know when someone is lying to me. And I know the Shanahans long enough too. They're always plotting and scheming but they're not bad lads. And I know from the look in your eyes that you're a good guy too!"

Cathal was delighted to hear those words.

"A good guy?" he thought to himself. "Nice!"

Daisy handed the reins back to Cathal, who led Paddy into the school for the rehearsal, which all went very smoothly, with The Master even changing the role of the three boys back to being The Three Wise Men with their traditional gifts, instead of being The Three Unwise Convicts.

"Obviously someone has given him legal advice that he wouldn't get away with labelling us as criminals," whispered Billy to Cathal, when The Master announced the change of script.

When lunchtime arrived, Billy, Barty and Cathal sat in detention again while the others left the classroom. Cathal thought about telling them about Granda's decision to send him away and about him forbidding Cathal from spending time with them, but decided that later would do. He also considered telling them about the beautiful orange light that he had seen from his bedroom and the subsequent vivid dream that he experienced about being in Murphy's Woods, but again, decided to wait for a more appropriate time.

"I hope Paddy'll be okay out there," remarked Barty.

"He'll be fine," said Cathal. "Daisy is looking after him."

"Oh Daisy is looking after him Barty," teased Billy. "Did you hear that?"

"Big deal guys, get over it!" replied Cathal dismissively. "Anyway, not changing the subject or anything but how much studying have ye done for this afternoon's exam?"

"I've done a bit," replied Billy, explaining that it was a long standing tradition on the final afternoon before the Christmas break for The Master to issue each class with a list of one hundred short questions across all subjects.

"Have you done much Barty?" inquired Cathal.

"Let's just say, I'm very confident of my best ever result," declared Barty with a smug look on his face.

"I wouldn't be too confident if I were you," said Billy. "I haven't seen you do too much studying, bar a few hours on Google last night."

Barty laughed before reaching into his school bag and producing the exam paper that he had taken from The Master's office earlier in the week.

"Read it and weep boys," said Barty, showing the paper to Billy and Cathal, with all the correct answers written into the answer spaces.

"So?" asked Billy.

"So what?" asked Barty. "This is the exam paper. I've got all the right answers so all I'll have to do is write them in or, if I get stuck, I'll just hand this one up!"

"That's cheating Barty!" declared Cathal, clearly not impressed with his plan.

"No it's not," interrupted Billy. "I think the more appropriate word is stupid."

"Ah, the two of ye are only jealous because I'm going to get the best result in the school, and you two will probably end up somewhere in the mid-table places!"

Billy took another look at the paper and a broad smile came to his face.

"Ya. It's definitely a very stupid move little brother!"

"How is it stupid Billy? You tell me."

"You see Barty, these questions all look very familiar to me," responded Billy. "In fact, they're so familiar that I can confidently say that this is exactly the same exam that I sat when I was in fifth class. The bad news for you is that The Master changes the exam every year without fail, so if I were you, I'd get studying because this is an old exam paper!"

The smile quickly disappeared from Barty's face, as Cathal and Billy both laughed heartily.

"Told you cheating wouldn't pay!" said Cathal, as Barty desperately rooted through his bag in a last ditch attempt to begin revising for the exam, which was due to begin in less than twenty minutes.

Meanwhile, in the school yard, Daisy McCathy had been taking good care of Paddy, walking him around the yard and ensuring that all the children treated him gently and kindly. That changed when the school bully, Ivan O'Toole, grabbed the reins off of Daisy and jumped up on Paddy's back, kicking his sides in an attempt to get the poor animal to run. Try as Ivan might, however, Paddy would not budge from the place where he stood. Daisy tried her best to wrestle the reins back off of Ivan but he was just too strong for her, and after a brief struggle, Ivan pushed her to the ground, with Ivan's accomplices laughing at Daisy, as she started to cry.

Ivan kicked Paddy again, but there was no reaction from the passive donkey until, finally, Ivan opened his palm and slapped Paddy on the side of the head. With that, the donkey darted faster than he had ever ran in his life, with Ivan hanging on desperately to the reins, a terrified look on his face as he struggled to stay aboard. Paddy ran like the wind all around the school, with Ivan crying like a baby as Paddy completed his first lap of the yard. Another lap of the school completed and Ivan was now panic-stricken on the donkey's back. Paddy galloped and galloped and reached his fastest speed as he approached the large compost heap at the back of the school. Then, as suddenly as he had started, Paddy came to an immediate halt, catapulting Ivan over his head, landing him face first into the stinking heap of rotting food waste and grass cuttings.

Everyone in the school yard ran to the scene, as Ivan emerged from the compost heap, covered from head to toe in the vilest smelling and stickiest type of waste imaginable. Ivan walked away in humiliation amidst torrents of laughter from the onlookers, the horrible smell following him. Paddy trotted back to Daisy and gave her a big lick on the cheek, as she smiled and led him back to the front of the school. The donkey was breathless but it was clear that he had enjoyed his exercise.

"Good boy Paddy," she whispered in to his ear, as Paddy neighed loudly, as if boasting about his victory. Ivan stayed well away from Paddy after that.

Friday afternoon passed quickly, with the exam taking up most of the time. When the time came to hand up the completed papers, most of the students looked happy with their work, with the notable exception being one Barty Shanahan, who left many blank spaces on his answer sheet. Before the children left the classroom for the Christmas holidays, The Master warned them all to be at the Community Hall a half an hour before the commencement of the concert the following night.

On arriving home, Granda was sitting at the table waiting for Cathal, who fed and watered Paddy before entering the house.

"We've a lot to talk about Cathal," said Granda. "Sit down."

Cathal took off his coat and laid his school bag on the floor.

"I made a few calls today Cathal, and met a few people, and it looks like there's a family in Cork who'd be happy to take you into foster care. They'll be here for you on Monday."

CHAPTER 18
ALRIGHT ON
THE NIGHT

The large sign outside the Community Hall read:

Ballycastle Christmas Concert

Fix our Roof Fundraiser

Saturday @8pm (sharpish)

The local people streamed into the hall and by 8pm, very few seats remained unfilled. Backstage, the children of St. Joseph's National School were busy putting final preparations in place for the big performance.

At about 8.15pm, the hall now packed to capacity, slightly behind schedule, The Master took to the stage in front of the closed curtain to a less than enthusiastic applause from the audience.

"Ladies and gentlemen, boy and girls, welcome to the Ballycastle Christmas Concert. We're all here tonight to help fix the hole in the church roof and all the money raised here tonight will go towards that very good cause."

There was light applause.

"Before we begin, I want to acknowledge the role of a few people in getting this night ready. Firstly, I myself put in a huge amount of work into getting the best out of the children, and some of them are challenging to say the least!"

The Master paused to allow time for applause, but only a highly awkward silence from the audience met his comments.

"Secondly, I'd like to acknowledge the work of my colleague, Miss O'Shea, for her part in preparing for tonight."

The audience gave a rapturous round of applause, which The Master clearly did not like, the false smile that had so far been etched across his face quickly disappearing. He continued.

"Okay, quiet please. Right, let's get on with it. Ladies and gentlemen, I give you the St Jospeh's National School, Ballycastle, Christmas Concert."

The curtain opened to further applause, with the younger children, under the charge of Miss O'Shea, being the first to perform. Everything was going according to plan and the younger children were delighted with themselves when the audience cheered after their performance.

Backstage, Cathal, Billy and Barty, also known as The Three Wise Men, were making sure that they had everything in order for their appearance, with Billy in particular getting ready to recite a poem that he had penned especially for the occasion. Paddy was backstage with them, enjoying the buzz of the occasion and getting plenty of attention from Daisy McCarthy and her friends.

As their scene approached, Cathal's mind was elsewhere though. It had been a terrible week for him, and now just a few days before Christmas, he was mentally preparing himself to move to yet another home, his fourth in two months. This would be the worst move of all he imagined, as this was his own grandfather giving up on him. He thought about how happy he used to be at home with his parents until it all went so tragically wrong, and wondered what he had done to deserve such a horrible sequence of events. He also hadn't told the Shanahans about the move and wondered how he was going to do that, knowing that they would be very upset to hear it.

Earlier that day, Cathal had confronted Granda for one last time about how he had rejected his own grandson, and about how Cathal felt betrayed by Granda's plans to send him to foster care. Granda got very upset and the two argued bitterly again, with Cathal maintaining his innocence and Granda maintaining his belief that Cathal was lying. Granda left the house in a temper and hadn't returned by the time Cathal left for the concert.

"Come on Cathal, that's our cue," whispered Billy to Cathal, who was so deep in thought that he hadn't noticed Billy and Barty walking on stage and now Billy was turning back to get the third wise man, to cries of laughter from the audience, most of whom thought it was part of the script!

Cathal followed the boys on to the stage with a completely dazed look on his face. In front of the Three Wise Men, The Virgin Mary, played by Daisy McCarthy, sat on a stool beside the manger, with Joseph, played by Ivan O'Toole looking on. Paddy, stood over the manger and Daisy had a hold of his reins. The Three Wise Men had the simple task of placing their gifts beside the manger and moving to the side, which Billy and Barty proceeded to do, but just as Cathal approached, Paddy lifted his tail and began to drop copious amounts of donkey excrement onto the stage and onto the head of Ivan O'Toole, who was seated directly underneath the donkey's rear end. The audience erupted into torrents of laughter, and everyone on stage lost complete control of themselves too. Ivan stood up, donkey droppings falling off of him and ran off the stage. For the second time in two days, Paddy had humiliated him, giving him a taste of the type of feeling that he himself frequently dished out to his own bullying victims.

When order was restored, Billy stepped forward to the microphone to recite his poem, *The Last Christmas*. Silence fell over the hall as Billy delivered the lines of a poignant poem that had clearly been written about his late father. Looking out to the audience as Billy spoke, Cathal noticed a distinctive bald head at the back of the hall. On closer inspection, he realised it was Granda. He was amazed that he had come at all, and for a moment was delighted, until he remembered his own impending departure. Barty was looking out to the audience too, and was moved to notice his mother wipe tears from her eyes as she listened to Billy's poem. Then Barty noticed another familiar face.

"No way, it couldn't be?" he thought to himself. He looked again and was certain as to the identity of the man.

As soon as Billy finished his poem, The Master came back on stage to make a final announcement before bringing the evening's proceedings to a close.

"Ladies and gentlemen, boys and girls, before we all rise for the National Anthem, I want to announce that the final amount raised here tonight between the entrance fee and the raffle came to €2,560. Thanks very much to everyone. Fr. O'Rourke will be delighted to take that money back to the presbytery tonight and add it to the roof repair fund."

As The Master spoke, Barty whispered to Billy and Cathal to take notice of the man at the back of the hall. Cathal did not recognise him at all, but Billy immediately knew him. When The Master made the announcement about the amount of money raised, the man at the back of the hall left abruptly, hurrying through the crowd towards the exit. The National Anthem started, but Billy and Barty were desperate to get off stage to pursue the man. With one line left in the anthem, they rushed off the stage, bringing Cathal with them. The three boys exited to the carpark through the stage door, just in time to see the man pull away in the same van that he used to deliver the stolen items three nights earlier.

"That's him, that's the guy who robbed Mrs. Murphy," shouted Billy, looking around and seeing a bicycle parked against the wall of the Community Hall. "I'm going after him!"

Before any of the others had a chance to say or do anything, Billy took off as fast as he could on the bike in pursuit of the van, with only a very dim lamp lighting the road in front of him. He could see the tail lights of the van in the darkness ahead and then noticed the van turning off the road onto a narrow dead end bohereen. This was the laneway to the presbytery, where Fr. O'Rourke lived alone.

Billy turned off the bicycle lamp when he got on to the bohereen, and as he reached the presbytery gates, dismounted and continued on foot, sneaking in through the garden and eventually reaching the rear of the big old house, where he noticed the van parked in the darkness. Inside the van, the man was barely visible, sitting alone in the driver's seat. Billy hid amongst the trees and waited.

Meanwhile, the Community Hall was full of excitement after the concert. It had been a highly successful fundraising effort. Cathal thought about running after Billy, but then thought it better to seek help, and there was one man in particular that he hoped he could ask. He ran back into the hall and hurried through the crowd to where Granda was still standing at the back of the hall.

"Granda," cried Cathal as he drew close, hoping to alert the old man to the crisis, but Granda was more preoccupied with mending fences.

"Cathal boy," responded Granda. "Look, I've been doing a lot of thinking and I don't know what came over me to be thinking about sending you away."

"That's great Granda, but we don't have time to discuss that now," interrupted Cathal, pleasantly shocked to hear such a change of attitude, but not losing focus on his immediate task. "Something major is happening. Just come with me and I'll explain it all."

Granda was confused and didn't know what to say or do, but as Cathal was so insistent, he followed his grandson outside.

McCarthy's Bar

CHAPTER 19
WHAT BILLY DID

Fr. O'Rourke was driving back to the Presbytery when he took notice of the unusual sight of a boy riding a donkey at speed along the road in the darkness. Continuing past the duo, Fr. O'Rourke arrived in the front yard of the Presbytery, where he parked his car, took out the bag of concert money and made his way up the steps to the front door. He was just turning the key to unlock the door of the house when he heard a voice scream out his name!

"Watch out Fr. O'Rourke!" shouted Billy, just as the misfortunate cleric received a terribly hard blow to the back of his head, which knocked him to the ground, his possessions falling to the ground with him.

Before Fr. O'Rourke even knew what was going on, the bag of money was gone and the assailant was making his escape. Billy had been observing the raider as he approached Fr. O'Rourke, and tried to shout a warning to the priest, but it was too late to prevent the assault. It was all over in a matter of seconds, but Fr. O'Rourke still had the wherewithal to activate the personal alarm device that he carried on him at all times. Pressing the button on the device sent an instant distress signal to the local Garda station and two other people living nearby.

Billy raced to the aid of Fr. O'Rourke, who lay bleeding on the ground, while the raider's van sped away from the rear of the house, out the front gate and onto the bohereen towards Ballycastle. Billy took off his jumper and placed it under Fr. O'Rourke's head, to help stop the flow of blood, and to make him more comfortable as he lay on the cold doorstep. Then, turning the key that was still stuck in the lock of the door, Billy ran inside and emerged a few seconds later with a blanket, which he draped over Fr. O'Rourke to keep him warm.

"God bless you son, whoever you are," muttered the dazed priest in appreciation of Billy's help. "The guards should be on their way now."

As soon as Billy heard mention of the guards, he immediately became concerned for himself.

"This isn't good," Billy thought. "Here I am, already charged with multiple crimes, with a dazed old man that's just been robbed, who probably won't remember any of this, and I've literally got blood on my hands, and the guards are on their way. I'd better get out of here before they blame me for all of this too."

"Okay, the guards will look after you Father," assured Billy, before running down the steps and out the driveway of the presbytery to where he had concealed the bicycle.

He cycled as fast as he could along the narrow bohereen towards the turnoff from the main road, and had almost reached the junction when the Garda patrol car sped around the corner, screeching to a halt right in front of him. Billy stopped on the spot, lifting his hands above his head in a signal of surrender.

CHAPTER 20
WHAT BARTY DID

After Billy left the hall on the bicycle in pursuit of the van, and with Cathal having gone back into the hall to seek help from Granda, Barty had an idea. Within a few seconds, he had brought Paddy out through the stage door before straddling himself over the donkey and galloping into the darkness in pursuit of the van, and his brother. By the time Barty and Paddy made it onto the road, there was no sign of any other vehicle or no sign of Billy. Barty decided to proceed towards Ballycastle Village regardless, since that was the general direction towards which the others had travelled. Eventually, one vehicle approached Barty and Paddy from behind as they galloped along, with Barty recognising the car as it overtook them to be that of Fr. O'Rourke. This was confirmed in Barty's mind when he saw the car turn off onto the small bohereen leading to the presbytery. Passing the bohereen, Barty decided to keep going as far as the village, where he would phone the Gardaí from McCarthy's Bar if he couldn't find Billy.

As they approached the outskirts of the village, the streetlights lit the way for Barty, as a tiring Paddy began to slow. Reaching the narrow old stone bridge near McCarthy's Bar, Barty heard a vehicle approaching at high speed from behind him. Turning to look, to his amazement, he saw that it was Cathal's grandfather in his old *Carina*, with Cathal in the passenger seat. Barty had never seen Mick Kavanagh drive any faster than 50 kilometres per hour, but obviously this situation had aroused a sense of urgency in the man. The car came to a halt when it reached Paddy & Barty. Cathal rolled down his window and called out.

"Any sign of them Barty?"

"No Cathal. I don't know where they are. They must have gone on further."

"Okay. You call the guards and we'll drive on further to see if we can catch up to Billy."

With that, Granda and Cathal sped away beyond Ballycastle Village, while Barty dismounted from Paddy, tying him to a telephone pole outside McCarthy's Bar, before rushing inside to ask Mossie MCarthy to phone the Gardaí to alert them that there was a robber in the area.

CHAPTER 21
WHAT GARDA JIM DID

Garda Jim O'Sullivan was having a quiet and peaceful Saturday night. Driving between Killcrown and Ballycastle, all appeared normal, with driving conditions being good and the roads being quiet. He was hoping that the rest of his shift would remain that way, but his hopes evaporated when his colleague back at Killcrown station radioed him.

"Attention, Jim do you read me. Over?"

"Jim here. Over."

"Jim, we've a panic alarm alert from the presbytery in Ballycastle. Not like Fr. O'Rourke to use it unless it's serious. Can you check it out? Over."

"I'm on the way. Over."

"Good man Jim. Let us know if you need back up. Over."

Garda Jim was just a few miles away from the presbytery, and knowing the roads so well, he would be there in a few minutes. He accelerated as fast as the patrol car would take him. Along the way, the road was really quiet. Just before entering Ballycastle Village, he met one vehicle travelling in the opposite direction, which seemed to be speeding, but Jim thought that it was his own speed that made the other vehicle appear faster. Driving past McCarthy's Bar, for a second he thought that he saw a donkey tied up outside the bar but was travelling so fast that he was gone too far to double check it in his rear view mirrors.

"It must have been a Christmas decoration or something like that!" he thought to himself.

Leaving Ballycastle Village, Jim met a van travelling against him, and not recognising it, wondered if it was up to any malice. He radioed his colleagues.

"A white *Toyota Hiace* van, 2004, Limerick registration, travelling from Ballycastle towards Killcrown if any units are free, check it out. May be nothing but check it out just in case. Over."

"Roger Jim. Unit on the way. Over."

"Also, met some fella in what I think was a saloon car clipping along nicely just before that, so keep an eye out for that. Over."

"Roger Jim. Over."

Garda Jim continued towards the turnoff for the presbytery, and had just rounded the corner onto the bohereen when he met a teenage boy on a bicycle, stopped in the middle of the road, his hands in the air, with his palms covered in what appeared to be blood.

CHAPTER 22
WHAT GRANDA
& CATHAL DID

In less than a minute, the time it took them to leave the Community Hall and sit into the car, Cathal explained the situation to Granda, that the real thief had been at the hall, that he had left a few minutes earlier in the direction of Ballycastle, that Billy had gone after him on someone's bike, that he wasn't sure where Barty was and that this might be their last chance to catch the real criminal and clear their names. Granda started his old *Carina*, filling the air around the car with thick smoke before warning Cathal to "buckle up and hang on tight."

Cathal felt his body thrust back into his seat as Granda sped out of the carpark of the Community Hall and onto the road, sending gravel and stones flying into the air behind them.

"What I meant to say inside Cathal was that I'm sorry I was so severe with you all along," shouted Granda over the noise of the roaring engine, his eyes firmly fixed on the road ahead. "I rang Willie O'Brien myself this evening and even though he won't tell the truth to the guards, he did tell me that he put ye in touch with a man in Limerick. Whatever trouble you're in, we'll face it together. You're my only family now and I must have been mad to be thinking of letting you go. I'm just not very good at this parenting or guardianship craic!"

"That's okay Granda, I'm sorry too," shouted Cathal in reply, nervously holding on to the dashboard with his fingertips. "Just make sure you do a good job at the driving!"

The pair sped along the dark country road, passing the bohereen that led to the presbytery, unaware of the action that was unfolding there at that very time. As they approached Ballycastle Village, they saw a donkey galloping along the road ahead of them, with a boy riding it.

"That's Barty on Paddy Granda," shouted Cathal. "Pull over."

Granda braked hard and the old car shuddered to a halt as Cathal wound down the passenger window.

"Any sign of them Barty?"

"No Cathal. I don't know where they are. They must have gone on further."

"Ok. You call the guards and we'll drive on further to see if we can catch up to Billy."

Granda and Cathal rushed away, and soon Granda was travelling at near top speed. He slowed slightly when he saw the headlights of a car coming against them, and as the car passed, he and Cathal realised that it was a Garda patrol car.

"That was a Garda car Granda!" exclaimed Cathal.

"It was and all boy, and he was travelling fairly lively too!" replied Granda. "He's not going back there for the good of his health either."

"Turn around Granda!"

"I will boy. Hold on tight!"

CHAPTER 23
DONKEY & CHICKEN

Mossy McCarthy complied with Barty's request to phone the Gardaí, and the answering Garda informed Mossy that Gardaí would be on the scene very soon. Barty thanked Mossy for his help and went back outside to make sure that Paddy was alright, untying him from where he had left him.

Walking beside Paddy, Barty wondered what had happened to Billy, and how far he had chased the thief's van on his bicycle, thinking that he would have lost sight of him very soon. Then he worried that perhaps he was seen following the van and could have been abducted or worse. Whatever had happened, Barty was growing extremely anxious, but his anxiety levels heightened further the moment he saw a familiar white van approaching Ballycastle Village at high speed.

"That's the thief's van," thought Barty. "I must stop him!"

In an instant, Barty mounted Paddy's back and rode the donkey out to the middle of the road as the van drew nearer and nearer.

"He'll have to stop!" thought Barty, his heart pounding as his grip on Paddy's reins tightened, with Paddy and Barty staring straight into the headlamps of the oncoming vehicle. Paddy neighed loudly and Barty screamed at the top of his voice, closing his eyes in anticipation of the impact, but at the last moment, the driver slammed on the brakes, causing the van to swerve out of control, avoiding Barty and Paddy, but ploughing straight into the stone wall just outside McCarthy's Bar. Barty dismounted from Paddy, and as his feet returned to the ground, his legs felt like jelly underneath him, such was the fright he had got from putting himself in the direct path of the speeding van. As he approached the van, steam rising from the crumpled front section, Mossy McCarthy and a small group of customers came out to see what was happening, the impact having been audible inside the bar. The driver was dazed but not seriously injured, with just some minor cuts and a bump to his head, and now he was slowly unbuckling his seatbelt and opening the driver's door to get out of the van, having been unable to restart the engine.

"That's the man who robbed Mrs. Murphy !" shouted Barty to the group of onlookers, as the van driver took a small bag in his hand and emerged from the van. Mossy McCarthy quickly moved around the back of the van to block the man from escaping by cornering him in the v shaped space that now existed between the wall and the crashed van.

"You'll wait there 'til the guards arrive!" warned Mossy, but the thief was having none of it.

"Who's going to stop me? Get out of my way!" shouted the thief aggressively, reaching back into the van and producing a baseball bat, which he proceeded to swing wildly towards Mossy as he limped towards him, still carrying the small bag in his other hand. Mossy jumped back to protect himself, and the customers from the bar didn't dare challenge the fleeing man for fear of a wallop of the bat. Barty pulled Paddy well out of the man's way as he passed them, as he continued to brandish the baseball bat in a menacing manner.

"I should never have braked!" he angrily growled at Barty as he hobbled past.

As the lights from an approaching car came into sight, the thief shuffled towards the middle of the road, standing directly into the path of the oncoming vehicle, forcing it to come to a halt when it reached where he stood. The man had planned to hijack the car and use it as a getaway vehicle, but it quickly became apparent that he had picked the wrong driver to stop. As he made his way to the driver's door to force the driver out, the car suddenly reversed away from him at speed, before coming to a halt about ten metres away. The thief stood and stared at the headlamps, as the engine of the car revved and revved. Finally, the driver accelerated amidst a cloud of rubber and exhaust smoke.

"He'll never hit me!" thought the man, a millisecond before impacting with the front bumper, which knocked him to the ground, the bat flying in one direction and the small bag flying in another direction. With the man rolling in agony, the driver of the car and his passenger emerged to cheers from the onlookers.

"Well done Mick Kavanagh! Well done Cathal boy!" shouted Mossy McCarthy, as Granda opened the boot of his car and took out a length of rope, which he promptly used to tie the thief's wrists behind his back as he lay on the ground.

"You don't mess with the Kavanagh's bucko!" whispered Granda in the man's ear, as he tightened the knots on the rope.

Within a few moments, a Garda patrol car with two officers arrived on the scene, arresting the man and calling for an ambulance. The bag recovered at the scene contained the concert money that had been robbed from Fr. O'Rourke, and when the van was searched, the Gardaí recovered the very painting that was taken from the Murphy Mansion in the burglary a few days earlier.

Meanwhile, Garda Jim O'Sullivan, who had encountered Billy on the road near the presbytery, had placed the boy in the rear seat of the patrol car, from where Billy explained everything and begged Garda Jim to believe him. The validity of Billy's story was confirmed by the injured Fr. O'Rourke when Garda Jim arrived at the presbytery. Billy had been worried that the priest would not have been able to recall what had really happened, given the blow to the head that he received, but to Billy's pleasant surprise, Fr. O'Rourke was able to describe events in full detail. Garda Jim called for an ambulance for Fr. O'Rourke and waited with him, while his Garda colleagues captured the assailant. Billy, Garda Jim and Fr. O'Rourke gave a collective cheer of joy when the words: "Suspect has been apprehended" came over the Garda radio.

CHAPTER 24
PIECING THE CLUES TOGETHER

A larger than usual crowd showed up for Mass on Sunday morning. News of the dramatic events had spread like wildfire around Ballycastle, and everyone wanted to hear the precise details of what had happened. Despite his injuries, and having spent a few hours in the Accident and Emergency Department of the local hospital, Fr. O'Rourke showed up at the church at the usual time to celebrate Mass. With his head heavily bandaged, he took to the altar, and immediately deviated from the usual routine.

"My dear people, before I formally begin today's Mass, I want to thank a number of people who have had a very difficult week, and to whom we all owe a great deal. I'm referring to Billy and Barty Shanahan and Cathal Kavanagh. Could we give them a round of applause please?"

Everyone in the congregation clapped and cheered for the three boys, everyone except for Peggy Moore, who sat with her arms folded, a bold look plastered across her face. Barty, who was sitting with his brother in the very front seat, stood and faced the congregation when the applause rang out, and theatrically bowed in appreciation, provoking great laughter. Fr. O'Rourke continued:

"And I hope that all of us have learned a very valuable lesson this week too, that it is always highly dangerous to jump to conclusions, and that people always ought to be treated as innocent until proven guilty."

Billy looked around and made eye contact with Peggy Moore, who instantly looked the other way, as did The Master, who pretended not to see him.

When Mass was ended, the three boys gathered together in the church yard, where many people approached them and congratulated them on their successful quest for justice. Granda was also accepting plaudits from people, with the story of his apprehension of the thief being a major talking point.

After a brief visit to Ted Hanratty's shop to buy the newspaper and catch up on some gossip, Granda brought Cathal, Billy and Barty to McCarthy's Bar for Sunday lunch, which Mossy McCarthty provided free of charge in recognition of the service done to the community by all four.

During lunch, Cathal proceeded to relay the story of his experience of witnessing the beautiful orange light from his bedroom window a few nights earlier, and how it hovered over Murphy's Estate for as long as he looked. Billy and Barty were highly sceptical at first, with Barty even asking Cathal if he was taking any medication, but after some time, they began to realise that Cathal was being totally serious, and that all logical explanations as to the origin of the light were unfounded.

"So it's a ghost light is what you've concluded Cathal?" asked Billy finally.

"Without sounding foolish, yes. I think it's the real Seánín Solas."

"The real Seánín Solas?" asked Barty. "What do you mean?"

"Thursday night, after I saw the light, I lay into bed and fell asleep. As soon as I was asleep, I had the most real and vivid dream that I've ever had. It was so real that when I woke Friday morning, I had to think seriously about whether or not it had actually happened in real life. The really weird thing is that I had exactly the same dream again last night."

Cathal then told the story of how he dreamt that he had followed the light to Murphy's Woods, and how it disappeared into the ground where he saw the sad young man with piercing red eyes. He also told them of how he remembered finding a piece of cloth when they were replanting the trees in the woods, and that he was now wondering if that could have been part of the clothes that Micheál MacDiarmada was wearing when he was buried under the woods.

"Wow. That's a great story Cathal. You should write that down," mocked Barty.

"No, hang on a minute," interrupted Billy. "Go on, do you think that you seeing the light and your dream and the piece of cloth are all connected?"

"Yes. Absolutely. Think about it. A strange light has been seen by a small number of people over the years in Murphy's Woods. People explained it as being Seánín O'Connor, out patrolling his plantation, and later it was explained as being Seánín Solas, the ghost of Seánín O'Connor. All that while, there was a man murdered and buried in those same woods. Then, I find a piece of old cloth, similar to what he might have worn when he was buried."

"But that doesn't mean anything Cathal," said Barty, dismissively.

"Just hear me out. Think about this. A woman's fiancé is murdered and his body is dumped. The woman is heartbroken and dies, but neither he nor she is at rest because of the trauma of their deaths, and because they are separated for eternity."

"Unless we do something about it!" interrupted Granda, who had remained silent throughout the conversation, as he listened to and thought intensely about Cathal's theory on the phantom light.

"You know Cathal, I think you might be making sense about Seánín Solas not being who or what we always thought him to be," added Granda.

"Well, there's only one way to find out I think," replied Cathal.

"How's that?" asked Barty.

"We could always dig the precise place where I found the cloth and saw the light go into the ground in my dreams to see if the body of the soldier is buried there!"

"That's crazy," interrupted Billy. "You see a light, find a rag and have a few weird dreams, and all of a sudden you know where to find a body?"

"I wouldn't be so dismissive Billy," said Granda. "Call me a dreamer or a fantasist or whatever you like, but I think Cathal might just be one of those people who spirits in the other world use to communicate to the living world. He's also a direct descendent of the missing man."

"You don't believe that surely?" replied Billy.

"Billy, there are just some things we'll never understand," added Granda. "Did you hear that music last Saturday in the mansion Billy?"

"Yes."

"Can you explain what it was?"

"No."

"Is it possible that there is no logical explanation?"

"Well, yes, I suppose."

"Well. Don't be so dismissive of other things you don't understand either!"

"But Granda," intervened Cathal. "Realistically, how are we going to convince the guards to dig for the body based on my dream and seeing the light and finding the cloth? They'll surely laugh at us."

"Well, Cathal, I'll put it to you like this," explained Granda. "I'm going to sit down with Garda Jim this afternoon, and Jim is going to apologise to me for all the distress caused by their investigation, and the wrongful arrests and charges and all that. After that, he will ask me if there's anything that can be done to make up for all the bad stuff, and when he asks that, I'm going to tell him that I know where there's a body buried."

"And if he says no?" asked Barty.

"Then, I'll have to remind him of the little bottle of illegal spirits that he purchased from me a few weeks ago, and how it would be a shame for his Superintendent to hear about it! He won't be long getting his shovel then!"

The boys chuckled at Granda's plan, and later that day, Granda met with Garda Jim. After a brief discussion, a dig was organised for the following morning.

CHAPTER 25
CLOSURE

Cathal turned on the kitchen radio just in time for the morning news.

Good morning, you're listening to Kingdom FM, it's 8 o'clock on Christmas Eve, Tuesday, December 24th, 2013. Here is the news:

Gardaí in Killcrown yesterday evening discovered human remains, believed to date from the War of Independence, buried in a shallow grave in Murphy's Woods, Killcrown. While it is too early to confirm at this stage, Gardaí believe the remains to be those of disappeared soldier Micheál MacDiarmada, whose body was never found after he was captured and murdered by British forces in 1921. The search of the area came following an anonymous tip off to local Gardaí.

Cathal turned off the radio again and looked across the breakfast table at Granda, who had a broad smile on his face.

"Wow!" Cathal exclaimed. "That little piece of cloth was really a part of a dead soldier's clothes, and those dreams and that phantom light pointed to the body! Am I psychic or some sort of medium or what Granda? Why did I have those dreams and see those lights and not anyone else?"

"I've said it before and I'll say it again Cathal, I think it's just something we'll never understand!"

A million and one thoughts were rushing through Cathal's

head, about Micheál MacDiarmada and Lady Evelyn, about his parents and his brother, and about what his dreams meant. He wondered if he would see any more lights in the woods or have more strange dreams or hear the flute music again.

"All I know Cathal," said Granda, "is that your great-great granduncle would be very proud of you."

"I'm glad to have helped Granda. It's amazing the way there seems to be a reason for everything, and how the truth always seems to emerge in the end."

"That's true," agreed Granda. "Oh, I've only just remembered. We actually have a photograph of Micheál MacDiaramada hanging on the wall in this very room, and I never even thought of showing it to you. How could I have forgotten?"

Granda and Cathal rose to their feet and walked to the wall, where numerous old black and white and sepia photographs hung in small wooden frames. After a few seconds searching a very old group photograph, Granda located the man that he was looking for.

"There he is Cathal," said Granda, pointing to a face in the photograph. "That's the man you helped to find."

Cathal gazed at the image and instantly recognised the face to which Granda was pointing. It was unmistakably the exact same face that he had seen in his dreams.

EPILOGUE

On New Year 's Day, 2014, just a little over a week after his remains were found, following ninety two years beneath the soil of Murphy's Woods, Private Micheál MacDiarmada was laid to rest for eternity. He was buried by the side of the woman that he never got to marry. The strange light that had been seen by some in Murphy's Woods over the decades, and which was once believed to be the ghost known as Seánín Solas, was never seen again after the re-interment and the hauntingly beautiful music that had been heard over and over in the Murphy Mansion was never heard again from that day forward. For the people of Killcrown and Ballycastle, it was their last ever haunted winter.

ST. JOSEPH'S NS

CHRISTMAS FUNDRAISING CONCERT

PROGRAMME

BRENDAN GRIFFIN

Selection of Christmas Carols
– Juniors, Seniors, 1st & 2nd Classes – Miss M. O'Shea

Poetry Reading
– Paul Shaughnessy 1st Class

Christmas Morning by M O'Shea

He woke at six and out he leapt
From his warm bed. He'd hardly slept.
Then down the stairs without a sound,
His heart began to race and pound.

Going through the door of the front room
He tried his best not to assume.
With sleepy eyes and ruffled hair,
He smelt the pine tree in the air.

The room was still in winter's dark.
No fire had died out in the hearth.
He reached up high and flicked the light.
His face just lit up with delight.

He ran straight over to the tree
And gazed in awe on bended knees.
He'd dreamt of this for half the year
And with his joy there came a tear.

After all had been inspected
And batteries had been inserted,
He raced up stairs to Mom and Dad
To show them both the gifts he had.

They woke at once with all the noise
And naturally were so surprised
To see their boy and what he bore,
An angel at their bedroom door.

Interval / Raffle

Poetry Reading by Thomas Lynch - 4th Class

Lá 'le Stiofán by Seán Ó Luing

In the West, the morning rest is broken by the Boys.
Upon high seas, the fisherman can hear the ancient cries.
In a tree far from the quay, the Monarch rests in danger.
In a house without a voice a sleepless night is over.

Through the day the music plays on doorsteps,
streets and homes.
The wild Atlantic throws itself with fury as it foams.
The King in hiding from the death is
woken by the violence.
An exile for a single day goes on his way in silence.

The merry sight of coloured life reflects in every eye.
A longing for the land and earth infects a deep blue sky.
His crown floats to the frigid ground, unnoticed by the
strangers.
The den of fools is rich with jewels and once
again is sober.

Into the night the bard's alive with story, song and poem.
The North Star rests above the crests much closer
to the dome.
No burial of regal style or sailing to an island.
The strangers come with talk of guns to his
drunken annoyance.

Nativity Play

3rd 4th, 5th & 6th Classes – Master S. Ó Luing

Poetry Recital
– Billy Shanahan 6th Class

The Last Christmas by Billy Shanahan

His music aired across the fields.
The constant hush that never yields
Came through so crisp and sharp and clear
As Christmas died into the year.

An ember burnt out in the air.
His bag lay waiting on a chair.
A borrowed week had paid the fare.
His Christmas ended in despair.

He could not find the words to say
How much his being had to stay.
He'd meet the Kings along the way
And miss the gift of a twelfth day.

His last breath quenched the candle light
As Christmas passed into the night.

The National Anthem

Ends